TIM HARRIS
timharrisbooks.com

The Children's Bookshop
9481-8811
Beecroft

HARBOUR PUBLISHING HOUSE

First published by Harbour Publishing House 2015,
www.harbourpublishing.com.au

Reprinted 2015 (twice)
Reprinted 2016

Text Copyright © Tim Harris 2015

The moral rights of the writer and illustrator have been asserted.

All rights reserved. Without limiting the rights under copyright reserved above, no part of this publication may be reproduced, placed in a retrieval system, or transmitted in any form including the internet, electronic scanning, photocopying, or by any other means without the prior written permission of the copyright owners and the publisher of this work.

Emojis provided by emojione.com

ISBN 978 1 922134 57 8

National Library Cataloguing-in-Publication data

Author: Harris, Tim
Book Title: Painted Dogs & Doom Cakes / Tim Harris
Series: Harris, Tim. Exploding Endings; Vol 1.
ISBN: 978 1 922134 57 8 (Paperback)
Subject: Children's Stories
Short Stories
Dewy Number: A823.4

EXPLODING ENDINGS

Book One:
Painted Dogs & Doom Cakes

TIM HARRIS

FOR THE STUDENTS
I HAVE TAUGHT.

CONTENTS

THE TOP 79 EXCUSES FOR BEING LATE 7

NOT-SO-SMARTPHONE 21

PAGE WARS (PART 1) 49

DETENTION ATTENTION 63

THE CLEARING 85

BOOM POWDER 89

PAGE WARS (PART 2) 111

MURPHY'S CHOCOLATE CAKE 135

YOU GOT GOT 147

PSYCHO SWEET TOOTH SEAGULL 177

LAST LAUGH 188

THE TOP 79 EXCUSES FOR BEING LATE

1. I forgot where the classroom was.

2. I forget where the school was.

3. I'm not late, I'm actually early for tomorrow.

4. You usually just check the roll first thing in the morning. I'm here for learning, not regularities. Now that we've made that clear - hit me with your best lesson!

5. Better late than never.

6. The rooster next door didn't go off. But I did learn this great chicken recipe from the neighbours last night - you'd love it!

7. 'On time?' I thought you said, 'One at a time'.

8. The bus broke down. Yes, I know I walk to school, but I had to stop and check it all out. You should have seen the smoke coming out of the engine!

9. Daylight Savings got me again. I think I'll move to Queensland, Western Australia or the Northern Territory.

10. I'm sick of the ridiculous speed limits. 60… 50… 40! What's that? Lodge a formal complaint with the RTA and we'll take it from there.

11. My sneakers got a flat tyre and I had to replace my leaking shoelace. That doesn't make any sense, does it? Talk to Dad. He's the one who feeds me these sugary breakfasts. Whatever they do to my brain is his fault.

12. I had to stop walking and take a few rests. 63 of them to be precise.

13. It's a bit of a long story. I don't have time to tell it

as I am already late. Now, mark my presence and make it snappy!

14. You already called my name. You mustn't have heard me. *look at best friend and make him nod in agreement*

15. I had to finish watching a movie. Have you ever seen Lord of the Rings? Man, that thing just keeps on going.

16. I thought we were allowed to come and go as we please. This is not that sort of arrangement, is it?

17. I got lost in the woods.

18. Dad got all the red lights. It's not my fault he's colour-blind.

19. Perhaps the real issue is the fact you haven't taught us Time yet. Check your syllabus, teacher.

20. It's International Rock up to School Late Day!

21. When I was walking to school, an old lady

THIS WOULD BE A LOT QUICKER IF WE HAD QUAD BIKES

needed help crossing the road, so I helped her. She was very grateful and wanted to know how she could thank me. I told her she had thanked me enough because I was now late for maths.

22. I had to put clean clothes on. But first I had to wash them, put them out to dry, wait for them to dry, take them off the line, iron them and then dress into them. You don't need any washing done, do you?

23. Gooooooood morning to you too!

24. My watch is broken.

25. My alarm clock is broken.

26. All of the clocks in our house are broken.

27. We don't have any clocks in our house.

28. Please tell me, what is this word 'clock' you so speak of?

NO, I AM NOT LATE AT ALL

29. I was giving my friend a slow-motion replay of yesterday's walk to school.

30. I am not late. You will mark me as early. *wave hand in front of teacher's face like a Jedi Master*

31. The first will be last and the last will be first… and all that.

32. I forgot my homework and had to go back home to get it. The annoying thing was that I locked myself out. After the locksmith came, I locked myself in. Then I locked myself halfway through the door. I know, I know… I can't imagine how silly it must have looked.

33. The chain fell off my bike, got tangled in the spokes, dented the rim, bent the fork, damaged the front derailleur, snapped the brake cable, negatively altered the adjustment barrel, smashed the crank arm, bumped the chaining bolt, depressed the down tube, scratched the front dropout, broke the cassette and blew the saddle rail into smithereens.

34. My flight was delayed.

35. I am late because I am brushing up on my

Spanish. Sabía usted que uno de cada diez niños llegan tarde a la escuela cada día?

36. I got caught in a blizzard. (Outback residents only)

37. That's what tardiness is. I thought it was something you put on fish.

38. I got caught at the school crossing. I also got caught at a river crossing, livestock crossing, equestrian jump, hula hoop challenge and dangerous mountain pass. It was a bit like the mountain pass in Lord of the Rings. Have you ever seen Lord of the Rings? Man, that thing just keeps on going.

39. I've been here all along - look! *snatch teacher's pen and put a tick next to your name*

40. I had to send an email, but we've got a really slow internet connection. National Broadband Network issues and all that.

41. My skateboard took on a life of its own and forced me to do a detour. It may have been to the skate park, but I'll never disclose that type of information to you.

42. I'm an undercover agent from the Educational

Board of Studies Registry of Excellence in Classroom Practice and Other Schooling Stuff. That's right, I work for the E.B.S.R.E.C.P.O.S.S. and you pass. Thank you for marking the class role so diligently. *walk out of classroom as if never to return. Wait a few awkward moments for the teacher to call you back in, smile sheepishly and hope your attempt at humour will get you off the hook*

43. My compass broke and I ended up too far west.

44. I took a little longer with my hair. I'm trying to impress someone and it ain't you.

45. Three words: Nullarbor. Don't. Walk.

46. I slept in because I went to bed at 4am. How would you like it if you had to play computer games all night?

47. I got held up at the school office asking when your birthday is.

48. The train got derailed.

49. You'd be late too if you had to rock up to school every day. Yeah, yeah, I know you come to school every day too, but try looking at it from my angle.

50. Can I ask you to close your eyes for a moment? *rush to seat, unpack things and open book to correct page* Sorry, what was the question again? You said something about me being late? Ummm … hellloooooo? Lookie, lookie. *point to self*

51. I hitched a ride with a rather large snail.

52. I… am… raising… awareness… for… slow… eaters… and… have… to… do… everything… super… slowly. Would… you… like… to… sponsor… meeeeeeeeeeee?

53. I came to school by jetpack. It turned into this weird teleporter and took me to who knows where! Then it turned into a bad hog and kept leaping forward until it was hit by a missile. The jetpack gave me a dragon cuddle, killed a few scientists, scored some gold, dodged some zappers and hit the roof. All that effort and it only took me a couple of thousand metres. Some joyride!

54. I cooked a slow roast for breakfast.

55. We moved really far away and I didn't factor that in when planning my morning commute.

56. I helped rescue a cat that had become stuck in a tree. I climbed the tree and managed to get the cat down, but then I became stuck. I had to wait for the fire brigade to come and get me down. The cat didn't even say thanks.

57. I got frozen by an X-Men character and had to wait for the sun to thaw me out.

58. 'Am I here?' I thought you kept asking, 'Do you hear?' It seems I have scored lowly on both fronts.

59. I had to take a golden ring and drop it into a volcano at Mount Doom. It took me waaaaaaaaaaay too long.

GOODBYE, PRECIOUS

60. The old lady in front of me at the bakery paid for her bread in five cent pieces. You can't rush these things. After all that, she was five cents short.

61. My sister is on her L's and she drove to school. Contrary to what you might be thinking, no, she didn't drive super slowly. She got pulled over for speeding. The policeman took a long time writing out the speeding notice because his pen kept running out of ink.

62. My hang-glider got caught in a stiff cross-breeze and sent me a couple of kilometres off-track. The view was great, but I'll be walking to school tomorrow.

63. Good things take time. School is good, and getting here takes time.

64. Slow down and take a look at yourself. Is it worth living life at this fast pace? I'm trying to help you out here.

65. There was no wind. Can't sail with no wind.

66. The lollypop lady took an extraordinary amount of time before letting me cross the road. She's the one you should be pointing the finger at.

67. I was at a funeral. Ants have rights.

68. Is that what 'present' means? I thought you were asking for gifts. These double meaning words get me every time.

69. I had a seven course breakfast and I didn't want to get indigestion by eating too quickly.

70. It takes a lot of time when you're learning to shave. Thankfully, Dad's a good teacher. And a good patient. I'm not the greatest pupil though. It seems I've let down two adults today. Ha!

71. My rocket became stuck in orbit. The traffic up there is unbelievable.

72. My shoes fell apart as I was walking. I had to go to the shops and buy replacements. It took ages

finding an exact copy of my old shoes - worn souls and all!

73. I got stuck listening to Dad's record collection. This morning he played me the soundtrack to Lord of the Rings. Have you ever seen Lord of the Rings? Man, that thing just keeps on going.

74. I think I need a louder alarm. Caterpillars don't really cut it.

75. Want to hear a random excuse? The paint was neither on the lawn, nor the dishwashing liquid on the spatula. Bricks are not evaluated according to age. That is why I am late.

76. There was another huge protest blocking all the streets. It looks like One Direction is back in town. Gotta stop that band.

77. Please direct your accusing questions to my Personal Assistant. *point to Jim*

78. Believe it or not, I have no excuse. I simply woke up later than normal, took forever in the shower, forgot my bag and had to turn back for it, got caught at the pedestrian crossing and was picky when ordering my lunch from the canteen. I therefore arrived a good twenty-six minutes later than normal. So sue me.

79. I thought this was a dream. That's the last time I try flying an elephant to school! I should also probably put some clothes on.

NOT-SO-SMARTPHONE

ONE

Does anybody in your family have a fancy phone? A smartphone? If they do, you had better be careful.

When Dad first brought home his new smartphone, I thought it was pretty cool. It had all the latest gadgets on it; the internet, games, photos, apps, video, voice recorder - you name it. If it had been invented, it was on Dad's phone. Dad wouldn't let anybody else touch his phone at first. But one night, everything changed.

'What would you like to watch tonight, Phillip?' asked Mum as we plonked ourselves on the couch.

'The wrestling!' I cried excitedly.

I hardly ever got to choose the channel and I jumped at the chance to watch my favourite wrestlers in action. Bruce the Bruiser was my favourite. I loved the way he always lifted his opponents high above his head before slamming them to the ground. Bruce the Bruiser sure was great to watch.

'OK, Phillip,' said Mum, sounding a bit disappointed. I think she wanted to watch something with a little less jumping and throwing.

'Thanks, Mum,' I said, clicking the TV remote. I changed channels just in time to see Bruce the Bruiser enter the ring, ready for his next fight.

NOT-SO-SMARTPHONE

'What's this rubbish?' said Dad, walking into the living room. 'Phillip, I thought I told you not to watch the wrestling.'

He looked at the TV just as Bruce the Bruiser lifted his opponent above his head.

'And who in their right mind walks around in their underpants?' he added, shaking his head.

Just then, his new smartphone started to ring.

'I'd better take this call,' he said, leaving the living room.

Dad was always on the phone. He worked for the bank and took lots of important phone calls at night. Mum used to get cross at him for working so hard, but Dad said there was nothing he could do about it. Sometimes I think he wished he had a different job. He used to joke about being an actor, but Mum said that acting didn't pay the bills. Dad would always smile, but deep down I think he liked the idea of being on television.

I went back to watching the wrestling and Mum went back to shivering every time Bruce the Bruiser slammed his opponent.

Dad eventually came back to the living room and sat on the couch next to me. His new smartphone was in his hand. I was just about to point out to him that Bruce's underpants were actually shorts, when something strange happened. The television suddenly changed channels.

'Hey!' I protested. 'Turn it back to the wrestling!' I glared at Dad, annoyed he had switched programs. Bruce's underpants weren't that bad, were they?

'Wait a minute,' said Dad. 'This is *Actor Advice*. It's my favourite show. I had no idea it was on tonight. Thanks for putting it on, honey.'

He looked at my Mum.

'Don't look at me,' she said. 'I don't have the remote - Phillip does!'

It was true. I was holding the television remote. The strange thing was that I didn't press any buttons on it. Confused, I placed the remote onto the coffee table.

'Thanks, son,' said Dad, sounding surprised.

I crossed my arms and frowned as Dad wriggled comfortably onto the couch. There was no way I would be allowed to watch the wrestling now. Once Dad started watching *Actor Advice*, there was no chance of changing the channel.

He must have sensed my disappointment because he handed me his new smartphone.

'Perhaps you can find a game to play,' he suggested.

Just then, the television changed back to the wrestling.

'No thanks!' I said, quickly giving his phone back. 'I've got Bruce to watch!'

No sooner had I given the smartphone back to Dad when the TV changed channels again. It went back to *Actor Advice*.

'Wait a moment,' said Dad thoughtfully, looking at the phone. 'I think my new phone is changing the channels.'

He gave the phone back to me, and, sure enough, the wrestling came on again.

'How very brilliant,' said Mum. 'Can I have a turn?'

I handed the phone to her and a trivia show came on.

'Oh, my favourite!' she beamed. 'I haven't seen this show for weeks!'

Dad was very impressed. So was I. It was like the phone was able to read our minds and put our favourite shows on. But this was only the beginning. The very next night, the new smartphone showed us how powerful it *really* was.

TWO

'What time will Dad get home tonight?' I asked Mum as I quickly finished my cheese on toast. I couldn't wait to go to the TV room and try out the smartphone again. Dad had left the phone with us since he was in a big meeting and he knew how much we wanted to use it.

'He should be home in an hour or so, Phillip,'

replied Mum. 'He will have enough time to help you prepare for your maths test tomorrow.'

'Great,' I sighed, remembering the test. 'I forgot about that.'

'Maybe you should go and start studying now,' suggested Mum hopefully. 'That way you can show Dad what you've already done.'

'No way!' I objected. 'I'm watching Bruce the Bruiser. He's on in ten minutes!'

'I'm afraid that won't be happening,' said Mum more firmly. 'It's an important test and I think you should go and do some work for it.'

'But Mum-'
'No buts.'
'But you-'
'No buts.'
'But I-'
'No buts!'
'But Bruce-'
'NO BUTS!'

I closed my mouth in defeat. When Mum raised her voice there was no arguing. She wanted me to study, and study is what I would have to do.

I trudged slowly to my room and slumped myself down at my desk. I pulled out my maths textbook and stared blankly at the pages. Who would write such horrible books? The complicated number questions before me seemed to rise up from the page, slapping me in the brains. There was no way I could do these questions on my own. I really needed Dad's help. I sighed and began to draw a picture of Bruce the Bruiser on the side of the page.

'WOO HOO!' yelled Mum from the TV room. 'I got it right!'

I ignored her and continued sketching. I was onto Bruce's underpants and I had to get them just right.

'California!' yelled Mum a few minutes later. 'WOO HOO! I can't believe I knew that!'

I stopped drawing and listened. Something was getting Mum very excited.

'1936!' she said a few moments later. 'Yes! I got it right again! I'm on a roll!'

The last time Mum screamed so loudly was when I accidently set fire to the rug. Something was working her up and I had to find out what it was. I put my pencil on my desk and tiptoed down the hallway to the entrance of the TV room. Mum was sitting on the edge of the lounge, her face glued to the television. She was holding the smartphone in her hand.

'Dolphins!' she exclaimed.

A man's voice sounded from the television. 'And the answer is dolphins.'

'Yes!' exclaimed Mum, noticing me at the doorway. 'Phillip, you *must* come and watch – I'm on a roll!'

I didn't need an excuse to watch TV, so I sat down next to her. She was watching the trivia. A man in a suit asked the next question.

'What is the capital of-'

'Brisbane!' blurted Mum.

'Mum, he didn't even finish the question,' I said, slightly annoyed.

'The answer is, of course, Brisbane,' said the man on the show.

Mum's face broke into a broad smile.

'Woah...' I whispered. 'That was amazing.'

'Pineapples!' said Mum suddenly, as the man started the next question.

I stared closely at the TV.

'The answer is pineapples,' said the man on the quiz, just before a commercial break interrupted the show.

'I haven't got one wrong all night!' beamed Mum, turning to me. 'How is the maths going, Phillip?'

'I'm... *wrestling* with it,' I said, hinting at a change of channel. 'My brain is... *bruising* from all the work.'

Mum picked up on my hints and gave me an understanding look.

'You can watch as much as you want tomorrow night. But for now, you really should go back to the books. Plus, I want to keep watching this quiz! Maybe I should go on it one day!'

Just then, the smartphone began to ring. Mum answered it. It was Dad. She quickly handed the phone to me. 'Phillip, he wants to talk to you. Can you take the phone to your room? I don't want to miss any of the show.'

I took the phone and headed back down the hallway.

'Hi, Dad,' I said as I entered my room. 'How's it going?'

'The meeting is going overtime,' he replied. 'I won't be home in time to help you with your maths.'

My heart skipped a beat with the good news. I

was off the hook and wouldn't have to do any more studying.

'That's OK,' I replied, trying not to sound too relieved. 'I hope the meeting goes well. See you tomorrow.'

I ended the call and put the phone down next to my maths book. Life was good. Thanks to Dad's long meeting, I wouldn't have to do any more work.

I picked up my pencil and started to happily draw Bruce the Bruiser's feet when something unusual happened. For some reason, my eyes were drawn to a question in my maths book.

'Oh, that's an easy one,' I said quietly to myself. 'The answer is 89.'

I looked at the next question. It was easy too. I wrote the answer down and moved on to the next one.

'Piece of cake,' I said. '246.'

For some reason, the questions did not seem so hard any more. I could feel a strange energy inside my brain. I felt smart.

I quickly completed a few pages before something interrupted me. Mum was screaming at the TV again, although this time her yells were angry.

'AARRGGH!' boomed her voice down the hallway. 'Why are the questions so hard all of a sudden?'

I looked at the phone on my desk, a thought entering my mind. When Mum had the phone before, she was getting all of the quiz show answers right. But now that I had the phone, she was getting them wrong. I was the person getting all of the questions right. It was like the phone was also able to put answers in our heads.

I quickly checked my answers in the back of the maths book. Every single one was right. I opened up

to another page and answered and checked those questions as well. Again, everything was right, even though I had struggled with the content at school. The phone was making me smart.

I thought about the maths test. Somehow, I had to take the phone to school with me the next day. The test would be simple with this amazing technology in my pencil case.

There was only one problem - Dad would need the phone again the next day, so I had to think of a way to stop him from taking it.

I smiled to myself, a cunning plan forming in my mind.

THREE

The next morning Dad was looking very tired. The meeting at the bank had gone so late he got home after midnight.

'They want me to take the top job,' he sighed, sipping his coffee. 'I knew I should have gone into acting.'

'Why don't you just quit?' teased Mum, though I sensed there was truth in what she was saying. She had said before that she didn't want him to take on a more important job. I think she wanted him to spend more time with us.

'Phillip,' said Dad, looking at me and changing the topic. 'Where is my new phone? I need it today.'

'I put it in your briefcase,' I lied, trying not to look him in the eye. I slid a hand under the table and gently tapped my pocket, making sure the phone was still safely there.

'That's my boy,' said Dad, ruffling my hair and standing up. 'You do well in that maths test of yours. I'll see you tonight.'

The test was first thing in the morning and when I arrived at school, I made sure that everything was ready. I turned the phone onto silent mode and put it carefully into my pencil case. I had to make sure it was nice and close.

Miss Bate began handing out the tests and I sat back in my chair, smiling to myself. This would be easy.

In no time at all the smartphone began weaving its magic. I could feel its power bubbling through my brain. It felt just like it did the night before. I raced through the first page of the test in a few minutes and quickly turned to the next page. The sound of the paper turning over drew the attention of Jason, the boy who sat next to me.

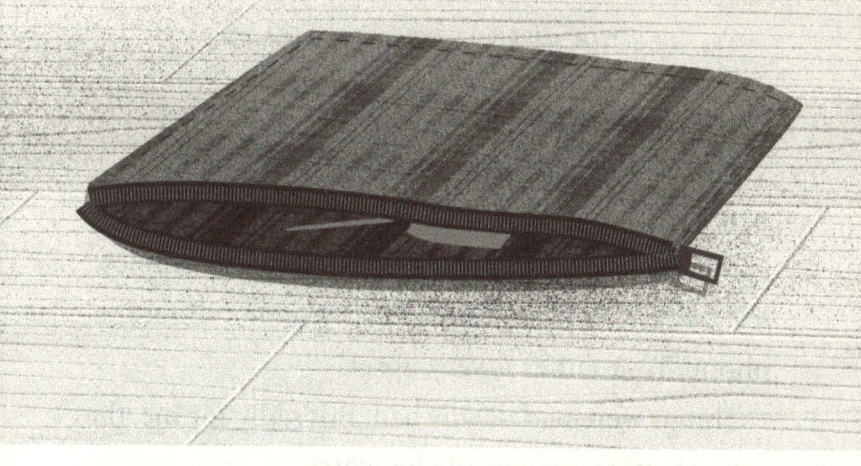

'Phillip,' he whispered. 'I made a mistake. Can I borrow your rubber?'

'Sure,' I whispered back.

Jason reached across for my pencil case and pulled it in front of him. I suddenly realised what was happening, but before I could react he had already noticed the phone.

'Woah!' he gasped. 'A new smartphone!'

He took the phone out and held it up, admiring it.

'Where did you get it?' he asked loudly, forgetting we were in the middle of a test.

'No talking, you two!' snapped Miss Bate. 'And you know the rule about phones at school, Phillip. Bring it here, please.'

My heart suddenly sank. Now I was in real trouble. Not only would the rest of the test be impossible, but Miss Bate would be sure to tell my parents about the phone. I sighed and took the phone to her desk.

At morning tea time, Miss Bate confirmed my worst fears.

'Phillip,' she said, flicking through my incomplete test booklet. 'I have emailed your parents about the phone. Your father is very upset.'

Things were bad. *Really* bad. But sadly for me, they were about to get a whole lot worse.

FOUR

Dad was furious.

'I can't believe you, Phillip!' he seethed. 'Not only did you take the phone, but you lied to me. That's the worst part!'

'I'm sorry, Dad. I-'

'Sorry doesn't cut it this time, mate! You are on washing up duty for a month!'

I dropped my head into my hands. I hated washing up. It was the worst job in the house. It also meant that I would not be able to watch the wrestling for a whole month, because washing up had to be done after dinner and that's when it was on TV. What a horrible punishment.

The next week was terrible. Every night was the

same old, boring story. We would sit together and eat dinner, then Mum and Dad would go off and watch TV while I cleaned the dishes. I could hear them cheering each other on as they took turns holding the phone to find the shows they wanted to watch. Dad was impressed with Mum's trivia skills. I don't think either of them worked out the phone was making her smart. Only I knew the true powers of the phone.

One night though, things were different. As I was washing up, I could hear Mum and Dad talking loudly during a commercial break.

'What! They're coming here?' protested Mum.

'They say that they need to do it here to understand my family life,' replied Dad.

'But job interviews should happen at work!' yelled Mum. 'The house is a mess!'

'We can clean it together... Phillip can help us.'

Now my ears were *really* burning.

'Why are you only telling me now?' complained Mum. 'It's just not fair!'

Mum burst into the kitchen, holding the phone. She slammed it onto the bench next to the washing up and gave me a frustrated glare.

'Make sure you wash up well, Phillip. Some men from the bank are coming home with your father tomorrow to interview him. They want him to take the top job.'

She suddenly looked sad. I could tell she was thinking about the extra hours Dad would have to work if he got the top job. She let out a deep breath, then disappeared into the bathroom to begin tidying up.

I went back to the washing up, but my mind was on Dad's job interview. What would Mum do if he got the top job? Would we see much of Dad at home?

I put a plate on the drying rack and then reached into the sink for the final object to wash up. The bubbles in the water made it hard to see what I was holding, so I tried to guess.

Hmmmm, that feels strange, I thought. *We haven't got any small plates like this.*

I scrubbed the side of the object, making sure it was nice and clean.

Maybe it's a new saucer for a cup of coffee.

I held it under the water and scrubbed the back of it.

It could be a coaster to put under cold drinks.

I thought I felt something sticky on it, so I left it to soak while I wiped the benches down. Then, coming back to the sink, I pulled the mystery object out. My heart suddenly froze when I realised what it was. It was the phone!

A massive shiver went through my body. Phones like this were not water proof. What if I had ruined it? Panic started to overcome me. I fumbled around madly, trying to wipe the wet bubbles off the phone. I pressed the ON button, hoping to find signs of life. Then, to my relief, the tiny power button lit up.

'Lucky!' I said out loud.

Without warning, something gripped the inside of my mind. I could feel it sweeping through my thoughts like a cold shower. I suddenly had the uncontrollable urge to smash something. I picked up a plate from the washing up rack and threw it onto the kitchen floor. It exploded into thousands of tiny pieces.

'WOO HOO!' I bellowed, reaching into the rack for a tea cup. I threw it wildly onto the floor and it smashed into smithereens. I jumped up and down and clapped my hands loudly. I was ready to smash anything I could get my hands on.

Dad ran into the kitchen and grabbed me by the arms.

'What on earth are you doing, Phillip!?'

The feeling left me just as quickly as it had come and I knew it must have been the phone. The washing up water must have gotten into the circuits. The phone was now sending out crazy thoughts and it made me smash the plate and cup.

'Quick, Dad, turn the phone off!' I yelled. 'It's going crazy! It's making me crazy!'

'Don't be ridiculous!' yelled Dad, snatching the phone off me. 'You're being absolutely idiotic. You're banned from my phone for a week!'

He powered the phone off and stormed away, clearly unimpressed with my crockery handling.

'Make sure you keep it turned off,' I said softly to myself, gazing at the mess on the kitchen floor.

Unfortunately for Dad, the next time he would turn it on would be the worst time of all.

FIVE

I was relieved to find out Dad had left the smartphone at home the next day. He was so nervous about the interview that he simply forgot to take it to work. Luckily, it was still switched off and it would not be able to get into anyone's mind.

School finished and I hurried home to start my punishment chores for breaking the dishes the night before.

I was raking up leaves in the front yard when the three men from the bank arrived home with Dad. They were all dressed in suits and looked very important. Dad was nervous about the interview and he wanted to make a good impression.

'How efficient to see your son working for you,' said one of the men as they walked to the front door. 'That's the sign of a good leader.'

'Well, that's actually a punishment,' said Dad, glaring at me.

'Good use of discipline,' said one of the other men.

Dad gave an official nod. It was interesting seeing him like this – his very best behaviour. Naturally, I wanted to see more.

As soon as they went inside I put the rake down and tiptoed over to one of the windows. I peered inside and watched as the three men sat down in the

NOT-SO-SMARTPHONE

living room opposite Dad. It was hard to hear what was being said, but it looked very serious and there was a lot of nodding going on.

Mum carried in a tray filled with afternoon tea and put it onto the coffee table. She took a small black device from the tray and put it in front of Dad. It was the phone.

Dad smiled and picked up the phone to show the other men. He pointed to the TV and waved his arms about. The men laughed and that seemed to relax Dad.

Then, Dad did something terrible. He turned the phone on. I gulped. I knew the phone had made me smash the plate and cup and now I was fearful of what it would do to Dad.

A strange look suddenly swept over him and he stood up. He gazed around the room with wild eyes and started shaking uncontrollably. The three men from the bank looked very confused and they began to frown.

Dad started singing like an opera singer and I could hear him through the window. His voice was loud and clear. He held the phone up high as he sang at the top of his voice.

'I LOVE YOOOOUUUUUU! YOU MAKE ME SMILE!'

The men were clearly shocked. This was no ordinary job interview!

Dad started twirling around, doing a ridiculous dance in front of them. He was acting completely out of his mind. The smartphone had taken hold of his brain and it was ruining the job interview.

He suddenly stopped dancing and leaped up onto the coffee table, kicking Mum's afternoon tea out onto the carpet. Bits of biscuit and tea sprayed across the living room floor.

One of the men pulled out his own mobile phone and started filming Dad's shocking behaviour. Dad seemed to like the extra attention and started acting like a chicken, flapping his arms wildly about and thrusting his neck backwards and forwards.

I couldn't believe what I was seeing. I don't think anybody could believe what they were seeing. Mum ran into the room and put her hands up to her cheeks, screaming. Dad wheeled around to face her, a crazed look in his eye. Mum screamed again and ran straight out of the room.

The man filming Dad on his mobile phone started laughing. The other two men were frowning and shaking their heads.

Dad dived off the coffee table and landed headfirst

on the couch. He started pretending to swim on the couch and began barking like a dog. Then he jumped up and ran out of the room, returning seconds later with a pair of his red underpants. He quickly put them on over his suit pants and jumped back onto the coffee table.

'I AM BRUCE THE BRUISER!' he bellowed, beating his chest. One of the men stood up to try and calm him down, but Dad grabbed him around the waist and lifted him above his head, just like Bruce would do. Another one of the men leaped up to protect his friend, but Dad kicked him out of the way. All the while, the third man was filming the whole thing on his mobile phone.

That was the last I ever saw of the smartphone. After I told Dad that I had dropped it into the washing up water, he threw it away.

Dad lost his job at the bank and he blamed the whole thing on the phone.

'It was like my whole brain was out of control,' he said. 'Now I know why you smashed the plate and cup, Phillip.'

While Dad was happy to throw the phone out, I was sad. I actually think the smartphone knew what it was doing all along. You see, the man from the bank who had filmed Dad's rampage, uploaded the video onto the internet. It quickly became a viral video and it was on all the websites and television shows. Dad could not even walk down the street without somebody recognising him.

A few days after the video had gone viral, Dad got a call from an acting agency that said they had been searching for someone with his looks for a long time. Dad was thrilled. So was Mum.

He now works part-time as an actor and makes more money than he did at the bank. Plus, Mum gets to see him all the time and so do I. And the best part is I can watch as much wrestling as I like. Dad says it is good for my imagination.

PAGE WARS I

IT IS A WELL-KNOWN FACT THAT THE LEFT PAGE IS FAR GREATER THAN THE RIGHT PAGE. THE LEFT PAGE IS, AND WILL ALWAYS BE, THE SUPERIOR SIDE OF A BOOK.

HUH? ... HANG ON!

WHAT ON EARTH ARE YOU ON ABOUT, LEFTY? YOU CAN'T JUST GO AROUND MAKING BOLD STATEMENTS LIKE THAT WITHOUT ANY EVIDENCE. SOUNDS LIKE A BUNCH OF STUPIDY-DUPIDY TO ME ... WEIRDO.

AND THIS INDEED IS MY POINT.
THERE IS NO SUCH WORD AS
"STUPIDY-DUPIDY".
THE LEFT PAGE NEVER RESORTS
TO SUCH CHILDISH LANGUAGE.

HA! CAUGHT OUT!

YOU JUST SAID,

"STUPIDY-DUPIDY".

NEVER RESORTS TO CHILDISH
LANGUAGE MY FOOT.

YOU DON'T EVEN HAVE A FOOT. AND EVEN IF YOU DID, YOU'D PROBABLY END UP KICKING YOURSELF UP THE BACKSIDE.

WHO SAYS I CAN'T HAVE A FOOT DRAWN ON THIS PAGE? I'VE GOT FRIENDS WITH PENS.

HEY TIM, COULD YOU PLEASE DRAW ME A FOOT? MAKE IT A BIG ONE. MAKE IT

A REALLY, REALLY BIG ONE.
CAN YOU AIM IT AT LEFTY FOR ME?

CHEERS!

OUCH! OUCH! OUCH!

TWO CAN PLAY AT THIS GAME, RIGHTY.
EVER HEARD OF A BLACK-OUT?

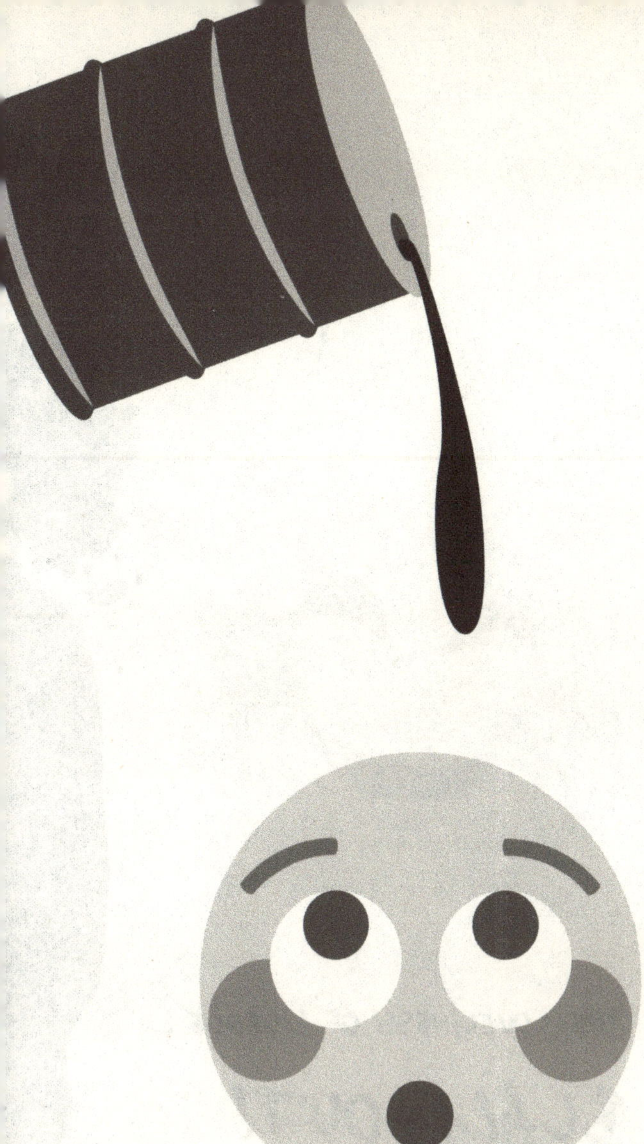

AH, THE LOVELINESS OF SILENCE...

BLACK-OUT!

I WISH I HAD THOUGHT OF THAT EARLIER.

AS I WAS SAYING,
IT IS A WELL-KNOWN FACT THAT THE LEFT PAGE IS FAR GREATER THAN THE RIGHT PAGE. THE LEFT PAGE IS, AND WILL ALWAYS BE, THE SUPERIOR SIDE OF A BOOK.

WHITE INK!

NOW WHO'S THE SMARTEST,
STUPIDY-DUPIDY!?

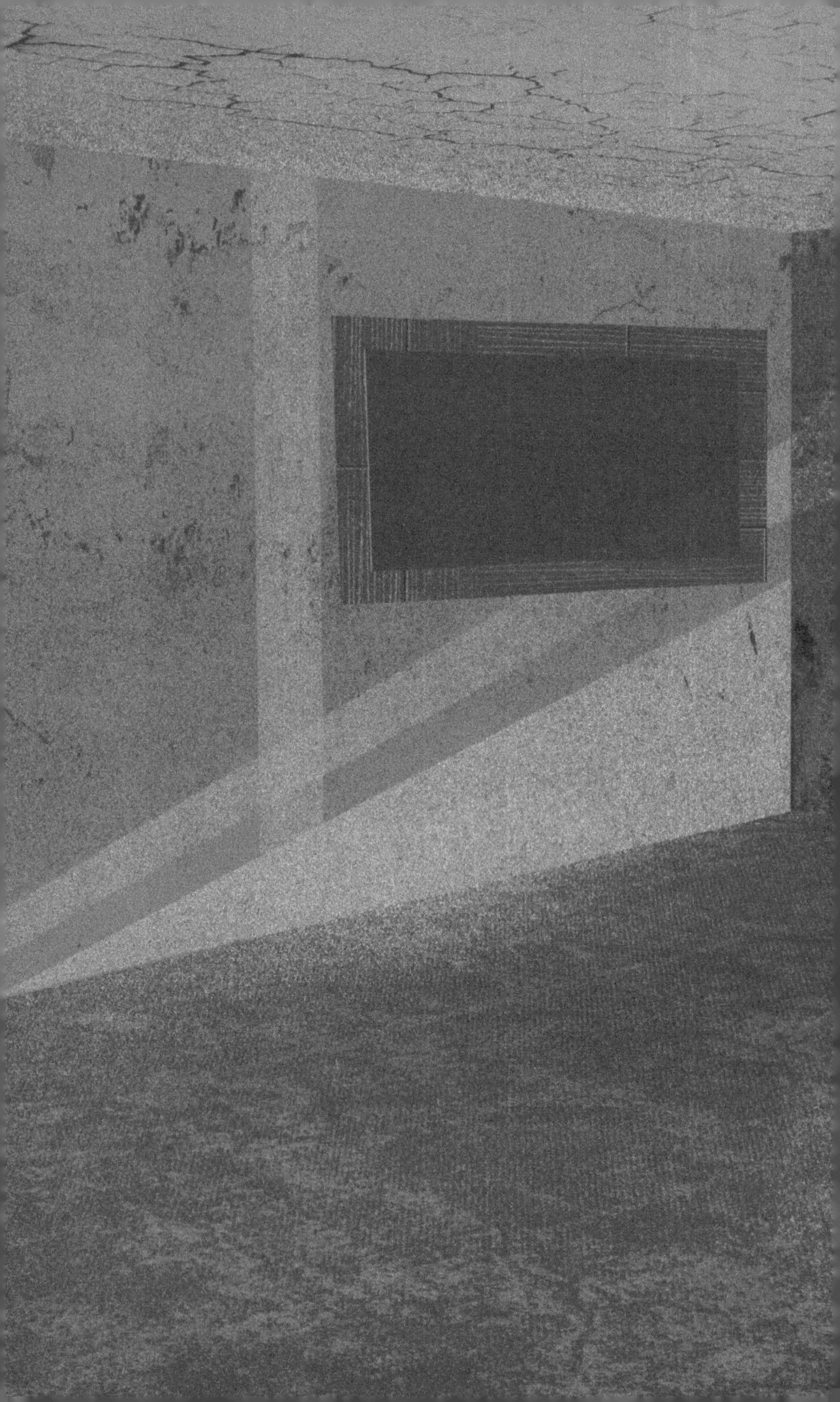

DETENTION ATTENTION

ONE

It has only ever happened once and I doubt it will happen again. Last year, at around 1 o'clock on 13th December, every single student at Milford Junior School was put on detention. Can you imagine that?

The day before the mass punishment, I was having my morning tea in the playground when Jimmy Webb raced up to me.

'Hi, Jimmy,' I said, biting into my apple. 'How's it going?'

'You'll never believe it!' he panted. 'Gavin's Gold! Think I found it!'

Jimmy was talking about Milford Junior School's greatest mystery. It was a mystery that nobody had been able to solve for a hundred years. Somewhere, hidden inside one of the school buildings, was a bag filled with gold - Gavin's Gold.

Mr Gavin, the first principal of the school, had inherited a huge amount of gold from a long, lost uncle. The strange thing was, rather than bank the gold, he hid it somewhere inside the school. But, as fate would have it, he died of a heart attack in his final year as principal without telling anyone where the gold was. For over a hundred years the students at Milford Junior School had tried to find the treasure. The kids still talked about it all the time but the teachers thought it was all a joke. I didn't think it was a joke and I wanted Gavin's Gold just as much as anybody else.

I stopped chewing my apple and looked at Jimmy, shocked.

'Really? Do you *really* think you found it?' I asked.

'I swear!' he puffed. 'The detention room… under the carpet… I think it's there!'

I liked Jimmy Webb. He was in my class, Fourth Grade. He was a friendly and likeable boy, but he had the unfortunate knack of getting into trouble all the time. He meant well and had a good heart, but poor old Jimmy was one of the few regular visitors to the detention room.

'You could be rich,' I said, taking another bite of my apple.

'I know!' he burst. 'So rich!'

I could not believe my luck. Was it possible that after all these years, I had the chance to get Gavin's Gold? I had to find out more and a plan started forming in my head. With Jimmy's help, it may just work.

'You had better be careful,' I said thoughtfully.

'What do you mean?' asked Jimmy suspiciously.

'Well, if you have *really* found Gavin's Gold, you don't want the whole school to know. Make sure you only tell people you can trust.'

He nodded in silent agreement, before turning and running off.

'See you back in class!' I called out after him.

Jimmy's words stayed with me during morning tea. I wandered around the playground, thinking hard. Not only was my head spinning with the news of Gavin's Gold, but Jimmy had reminded me I had to go to the detention room at lunch. I hated that room.

The detention room was the oldest building in the school. It stood by itself at the edge of the playground. Its brown, weathered walls mocked any student who dared go near it. Nobody enjoyed going there. Why would they? If you were silly enough to get a detention, it was absolute torture. There were no chairs or desks in the room and you simply had to sit on the dirty, worn carpet. There was nothing to do but stare at the grimy, old walls. Minutes seemed to last hours in that room. All the kids, and even the teachers, had grown to dislike the building more than anything else at Milford Junior School.

Today was different though. Today, I would go to the detention room with something else on my mind

– Gavin's Gold. The bell sounded and I headed back to class.

As soon as I entered the room, I saw Jimmy talking excitedly to his best friend, Dean Dallas. I walked over to him and tapped him on the shoulder.

'Be careful,' I reminded him. 'Not the whole school. Just the people you trust.'

TWO

The sound of the lunch bell filled the air. The time had come. Here was my chance to get Gavin's Gold. Feeling happy with my plan, I quickly made my way to the detention room and sat down on the old, stained carpet. The room smelt musty and the bare walls towered above me. But, today they didn't seem so bad. As I looked at them with fresh eyes, they seemed to glisten like Gavin's Gold might. I had treasure on my mind.

A Second Grade boy, Tommy Smith, suddenly poked his head through the door and looked at me, seeing if it was safe to come in. I nodded to him and he sat down nervously on the carpet next to me.

'What did you do to get a detention?' I whispered.

He looked anxiously around the frightful room before whispering back, 'Didn't do my homework. Third time in a row.'

We sat in silence, two lonely figures in the centre of the disgusting room. Lunch seemed to be dragging on for a lifetime. You could almost hear time passing. I could see why the students at Milford Junior School were so well behaved. Nobody in their right mind would want to spend their lunchtime - or anytime - in here.

My thoughts turned again to Gavin's Gold. What if Jimmy had really found out where the treasure was stored? Had he uncovered the great mystery? He *had* mentioned the carpet. Could it be here, hidden somewhere beneath me? I decided to look at the floor carefully, determined to find a clue.

It was toward the end of lunch that I eventually saw it. Near the front of the room, a single unravelled thread of carpet was poking up. The carpet was worn around the thread and it looked as though someone had been picking at it. I waited impatiently for the final lunch bell to sound before making my move.

The bell eventually rang and Tommy leaped to his feet and dashed outside. He clearly did not want to hang around. I crept to the front of the room, eager to take a closer look at the carpet. I pulled the thread by the end, unravelling it some more, before picking at a couple of bits of carpet around it. I wedged my smallest finger into a tiny hole that had formed around the base of the thread, and tore it open.

'That's it!' I exclaimed. My words echoed around the empty detention room. I had to tell Jimmy.

THREE

Jimmy buzzed with excitement when I told him later that afternoon. The class was doing a writing test.

'I knew it!' he whispered excitedly, trying not to draw attention to himself. 'I knew it was there. I can't believe you saw it too!'

A couple of students were looking at us, so Jimmy lowered his voice.

'I have to get in there today … after school.'

'No can do,' I replied. 'It's locked all day and all night. It is only ever open at lunch.'

'But…but… it could be worth millions,' he stammered. 'Billions… trillions…. gazillions!'

I shook my head. 'It will have to wait, Jimmy. The

DETENTION ATTENTION

only way to get into the room is to get a detention. And who wants to do that?'

'I do,' said Susan Poach. She had been listening in the whole time.

Susan Poach, with her freckles and ponytail, was the worst person to find out. Her nickname was Motor Mouth and she was famous for spreading secrets. Worst of all, she seemed to know everybody in the school and everybody in the school seemed to know her. It would be impossible to keep Gavin's Gold a secret now. Susan gave a mean smile and turned to the girl next to her, whispering immediately into her ear.

FOUR

The next morning the playground was buzzing. Everybody was talking about Gavin's Gold. Motor Mouth Susan had made sure of that. The students had gathered around the detention room and were chatting excitedly. One student was even standing at the door, peering through the key hole expectantly.

Mr Mallet, the Sixth Grade teacher, was on duty. He was one of the strictest teachers in the school and he stepped in to break up the crowd.

'What's this about?' he spluttered, stepping between the students and the building. 'Stop this nonsense! What's going on?'

'You look like a banana peel, sir! That's what's going on!' blurted out Derrick Barnes, a boy in Mallet's class.

Mr Mallet's jaw dropped. He could not believe what he had just heard.

'EXCUSE ME, BARNES!? He bellowed.

'You look like a big, fat banana peel, sir!' teased Derrick again. 'You heard me. A big, fat banana peel!'

Mr Mallet looked furious. You could almost see the anger steam coming out of his ears.

Derrick pretended to peel a banana and pointed

to the teacher. 'Banana peel,' he said again, this time poking his tongue out.

'DETENTION, BARNES!' roared Mr Mallet, looking frightfully angry.

Derrick Barnes' face spread into a cunning grin, though he tried to hide it. 'Excellent,' he said under his breath. He rubbed his hands together and looked at the detention room.

The gathering of students was shocked at Derrick's behaviour, but they knew what he was up to. He wanted to get into the detention room before anybody else. He was prepared to get into big trouble for the rich reward. The students looked around at each other and everybody was thinking the same thing – how to get a detention.

The bell rang and the students headed back to class. Nobody knew just how crazy things were about to get!

FIVE

Sixth Grade was the first grade to be put on detention. It only took them ten minutes. As soon as the morning lessons had started, Mr Mallet, who was still in a horrible mood, was already snapping and yelling at his students. All it took was the class to burst into song, singing, *'Mallet wears nappies, Mallet is a baby – Mallet wears nappies, Mallet is a baby'*, before the cranky teacher put the whole lot of them on detention.

The other Sixth Grade class soon heard the news. Not wanting to miss out on the chance to find Gavin's Gold, they quickly put their teacher to the test. They started jumping up onto the desks, acting like wild monkeys. They put their hands under their arms and made ridiculous monkey noises, poking their tongues out at the poor teacher. Moments later they had their reward – a whole class detention.

Third Grade followed shortly after.

DETENTION ATTENTION

The students in that class thought it would be a good idea to rip up their maths books. Bits of torn up paper with numbers were soon flying across the classroom in a huge paper fight. It made it look like it had been snowing. Their teacher was shocked at the outrageous behaviour and had no hesitation in getting them all in trouble. The Third Grade students later said that it was the best way to do it. Not only did they get their precious detention, they got out of maths that day too.

My class received detention during morning tea. Spurred on by the Grade Three and Six stories, and not wanting to miss out on the chance for gold, the Fourth Grade kids turned the playground into a battlefield of food. It was an edible warzone. Each student, armed with their morning tea, got involved in the largest food fight our school had ever seen. There were apple grenades and orange bombs, machine guns of grapes, booby traps of soft cheese and bullets of biscuits. It was a fun way to get into a lot of trouble.

The teachers looked shaken at the end of morning tea. Never in the history of the school had there been such naughty behaviour. The students were out of control and nobody knew what to do.

Shortly after the morning tea break, the Fifth Grade teacher's voice suddenly echoed down the corridor and drifted into our classroom.

'HOW DARE YOU! THE CLASSROOM IS NOT A BATHROOM! MR LAWLER'S OFFICE! NOW!'

One of the fifth grade boys trudged past our room on his way to the principal's office. He was smiling and muttering to himself, something about 'liquid gold' and 'worth it'. He ended up with a whole week of lunchtimes.

The Fifth Grade teacher had become so upset that she placed the rest of the class on detention for working too quietly. Go figure!

The youngest students were the last to go, but their detention was by far the most spectacular.

The Kindergarten, Grade One and Grade

Two teachers had taken their classes to the art room for some painting. They were to be doing Christmas art.

After listening carefully to the instructions, the students returned to their desks, ready to paint. However, painting their blank pieces of paper was the last thing on their mind. Armed with thick brushes and bright colours, they began to paint their desks as if they were blank canvases. The horrified teachers yelled at them to stop, but the children kept painting. They quickly finished painting their desks and then moved onto their chairs. Soon they were painting the walls and floor. The art room was turning into an art*work*. The teachers' desks were next, but what followed was the naughtiest of all. The teachers themselves were the target for a paint makeover. The screaming adults were quickly covered from head to toe in thick, sticky paint. The little kids giggled and laughed as they attacked the poor teachers with their paint brushes.

The noise soon drew the attention of the school principal, Mr Lawler, who burst into the room, before collapsing out of shock. Needless to say the giant Picasso earned every single one of them a detention.

Lunch was now minutes away and every student at Milford Junior School would soon be heading for the detention room. Their goal was accomplished and the only thing left to do was to find Gavin's Gold.

SIX

As soon as the first lunch bell sounded, I walked slowly to my bag and took out my lunch. Hundreds of crazed students were scrambling around me, each wanting to be the first to the detention room.

I sat on a seat outside my classroom and ate my sandwich, watching the race. There was no rush. I knew the treasure would be mine. A couple of slower Kindergarten kids bustled past, heading for the detention room. I picked up my drink bottle, took a big sip and looked at my watch. Five more minutes would do the trick.

As I walked across the playground to the detention room, the scene before me was extraordinary. Deafening screams of excitement filled the air. Students were tearing at the outside of the detention room with their bare hands, trying to pry open the wooden panels that lined the building.

Students of all ages were running in and out of the main door, screaming and yelling instructions at each other. Bits of carpet were being tossed through the open windows. I heard a loud crash inside and then some cheering. A large floorboard was dragged outside by a couple of boys in Sixth Grade.

I took a few small steps closer to the building. A group of girls in my class were kicking at the outside walls, smashing holes in the thin, wooden panels, desperately looking for Gavin's Gold.

I strolled casually into the doorway and looked inside. The room was a complete mess. It was like a shipwreck on dry ground that had also been hit by a bomb. Two bombs. Fifty bombs! Students were crawling over the floor, tearing at the carpet, ripping up greedy tufts of it with their bare hands. In an area where the carpet had been stripped, floorboards were showing.

In another part of the room, a couple of older students were kneeling around a gaping hole in the floor, thrusting their hands inside and feeling for any sign of the treasure. Some Third Grade students had kicked holes in one of the walls and were busily throwing the rubbish out through the windows. On the far side of the room, the younger students were jumping up and down, trying to make yet another hole in the floor. I took a deep breath. Now was the time to act.

'STOP RIGHT NOW!'

The students suddenly froze and looked at me, horrified.

'OUTSIDE! ALL OF YOU!' I yelled at the top of my voice.

I pointed to the door.

A look of shock suddenly swept over the students' faces. Nobody dared move. They looked around the room, realising how much trouble they were in. Every single student in the school had destroyed the old detention room.

A Kindergarten girl was the first to break the frozen scene. She ran up to me, hugging my leg.

'I'm sowwy, Mr Saunders,' she cried. 'Please don't tell my mummy and daddy.'

A Third Grade boy soon joined her.

'I'm so sorry, sir,' he said, offering his hand. 'It'll never happen again, I promise. Please don't get me into more trouble.'

'All of you outside, now!' I yelled again, pointing to the door.

One by one, the students tiptoed past me, aiming to avoid any more trouble. The room slowly emptied.

'Sorry, Mr Saunders,' said the girls in my class as they walked sadly past.

Jimmy Webb was the last one to leave the detention room. He stopped at the door and looked at me with big, watery eyes.

'Mr Saunders ... I ... errr ... well ... I ...'

'Outside!' I reminded him.

With the whole school lined up in the playground,

I voiced my disappointment.

'I am shocked and horrified,' I said, walking along the long row of frightened students. 'You have all behaved terribly. Poorly. Shockingly. Each and every one of you is on detention again tomorrow. *And* you are going to fix this mess!'

SEVEN

A few days later, Mr Lawler stood at the front of the staffroom with a glass of orange juice in his hand. It was the last day of school and the students had all gone home. It was the final meeting for us teachers before we got out for the summer.

'What a strange end to the year it was,' he said, taking a sip from his glass. 'I've never seen such bad behaviour from our students. I have no idea what could possibly have gotten into them. But still, a tradition is a tradition, and a prize is a prize. Mr Saunders, please come and accept your award.'

I walked proudly to the front of the staffroom and took a large, golden trophy from Mr Lawler. He shook my hand and turned to the other teachers, saying, 'Congratulations, Mr Saunders, winner of giving out the most detentions this year. The trophy is yours. You won it fair and square.'

The other teachers clapped. It was the first time I had won Gavin's Gold.

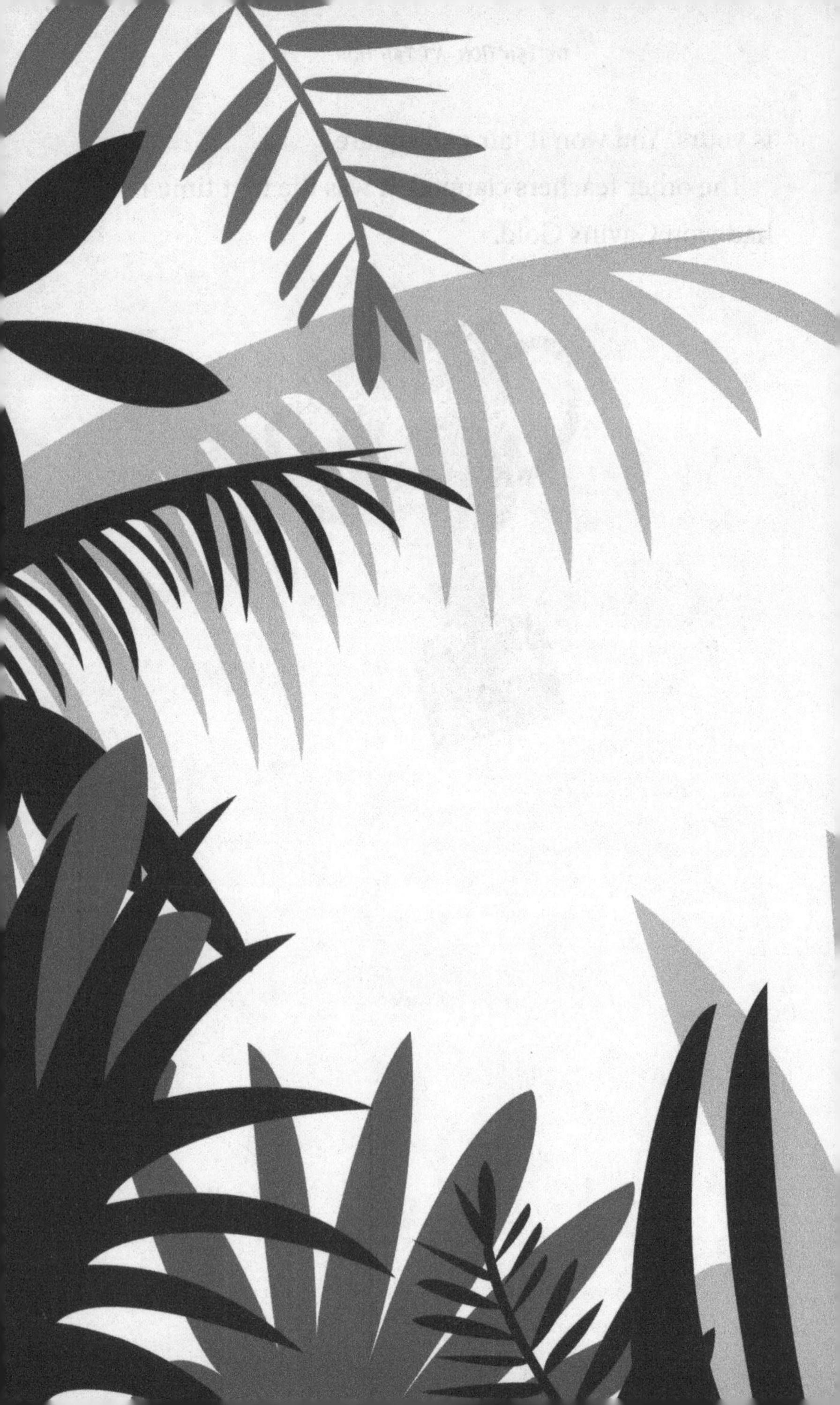

THE CLEARING

The clearing couldn't be far off. Olivia was certain of it. Her life depended on it.

She had been hacking for hours, cutting her way through the densest of forests, studying the map and following a steady south-east direction on her compass.

She had come this way before, though things had been different then. The path had been less wild. With time, she discovered, things had gotten worse.

Today, in the heat of the sun, she struggled forward, the knife slashing ahead of her, inching its way toward the precious clearing.

She paused for a drink, greedily taking in the final drops from her canteen.

Her heart sank. It was empty. It was as hollow as

the void in her stomach. She needed food and water and she needed them now. She needed the clearing. She had to make it.

Olivia's hopes were refuelled by a sound; a gentle whirring, teasing her ahead; the soft hums of a motor. She pushed on, always heading south-east.

Finally, when exhaustion and fatigue were at their most dangerous, she stumbled into a section of the landscape where the trees were sparse. She knew she was close.

Olivia mustered her final strength and made one

THE CLEARING

last burst, desperately slicing the few remaining vines. She was through. She had made it.

'There you are, lovely girl,' said Olivia's mother, stepping off the veranda and giving her a freshly blended juice. 'I made you a smoothie!'

Olivia gulped breathlessly at the drink, pausing only to utter something she should have said long ago. 'Tell … Dad …' she managed, 'he needs … to … cut the … lawn …'

Her mother gave a look of agreed frustration. 'I know, sweetie. It's a jungle out there.'

BOOM POWDER

ONE

I carefully tipped a teaspoon of Boom Powder inside the fuel tank. My science project was ready for its first test. I nodded to Dad, who stepped forward holding a box of matches. He leaned over the tiny rocket and lit the wick, before scurrying to join me behind the safety shield. We put our protective goggles on and started the countdown.

'10, 9, 8...'

The rocket began to gently tremble.

'7, 6, 5...'

There was a glimpse of flame. I held my breath and put my fingers in my ears.

'4, 3, 2...'

The miniature engine started to roar.

'1, zero!'

The rocket suddenly shuddered and let out an enormous puff of smoke. This was followed by silence. Nothing. It didn't launch. It didn't fly. It just sat on the grass, hopelessly grounded to earth.

I stepped out from behind the safety screen and voiced my disappointment.

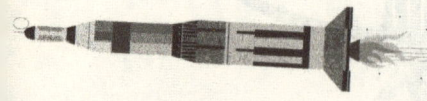

'Smoke! What a failure! What went wrong with the Boom Powder, Dad?'

'I'm not sure. It seemed to – WAIT! Clementine!'

Dad grabbed my arm and quickly pulled me back to safety. The rocket began to vibrate again, this time more violently. Streaks of flame sprayed out from underneath the engine, making the missile dance on the grass. It began to tilt to one side, then toppled over completely and shot straight over the back fence, just missing the washing line - into our neighbour's yard.

Dad and I looked at each other. We were in trouble now. The only thing worse than a failed rocket launch was having the rocket land in Mr Grimps' backyard. Mr Grimps was the meanest man in town. A real crank. If there was something to complain about, he would find it. If there was a chance to yell, he would take it. And if there was a child to blame, he would point at me. He was one horrible grouch.

There were only two things Mr Grimps loved more than being a bully. The first was his son, Blake. The second was his backyard — a backyard that had won several gardening competitions. A backyard that was now home to our rocket. Dad and I knew there would be trouble over this, so we tiptoed quietly up to the fence. We peered cautiously over the palings in search of our runaway missile, but Mr Grimps had beaten us to it. He stood in the middle of his neatly kept lawn with the rocket in his hands. He was already going red in the face and his fat moustache was trembling with anger.

'How dare you pollute my property!' he spluttered upon seeing us.

'Good afternoon,' said Dad politely. 'I see you found Clementine's experiment.'

'Not much of an experiment if you ask me! All you are doing is making more rubbish and mess!'

'Oh but there is no pollution in-'

'Rubbish and mess!'

Mr Grimps stomped over to a water tank on the edge of his lawn.

'How many times do I have to remind you, Collier,' he seethed at Dad. 'Nothing is allowed near the water tank. Nothing at all!'

With that, he snapped the rocket over his knee, breaking it in half. He threw the shattered space craft into his garden bin and stormed inside.

BOOM POWDER

Mr Grimps' son Blake was watching the whole thing, his nose pressed against a window at the back of the house. He poked his tongue out at me and then disappeared behind a curtain. And that was that... for now.

TWO

Mr Davis stood at the front of the classroom, greeting us with a smile.

'Come in, my young learners. Come in,' he said, winking at me as I took my seat. He was a big fan of my Boom Powder experiment.

'Now tell me,' he said, once the class was settled. 'how did part one of your experiments go?'

'Mine is already perfect!' announced Blake Grimps, showing off as usual.

'After just one test?' asked Mr Davis calmly. 'Tell me more.'

'All you need is good sunlight. It's so easy. Hook the solar panels up to the wheels and then connect the motors.'

Blake was good at boasting.

'Then set the motion sensors on the target – me! The tank will follow you everywhere.'

'But what's the point of that?' asked a girl from behind me. 'Why would you want a water tank following you around?'

A couple of other kids giggled.

'Don't you know anything!?' mocked Blake. 'People should only drink pure rain water. There is too much junk in everything else. Cordial is bad, soft drinks are bad. Even juice is bad. It all makes you go silly. My water tank gives you pure water whenever you want it.'

Blake was sounding just like his grumpy father. And this is the reason Mr Grimps was always so cranky when anything found its way into his backyard. He didn't want his precious water tank to have a hint of dirtiness. He didn't want his vegetable patch to have a hint of litter. He said that Blake was only allowed to eat natural things grown from natural conditions. But most of all, Blake was only allowed to drink pure rainwater.

'I see, I see,' said Mr Davis, turning to the girl next to me. 'What about you, Angie? What do you think we should be able to drink?'

'I disagree with Blake, sir. Other drinks are good too. I think lemonade is good because it-'

'Makes you silly and hypo!' interrupted Blake.

Mr Davis frowned.

'Well, I am inventing lemonade powder,' continued Angie, ignoring Blake. 'All you have to do is add the powder to water and presto - instant lemonade! Think of all the plastic you could save by not buying bottles and bottles of lemonade. One tiny teaspoon can make fifty bottles!'

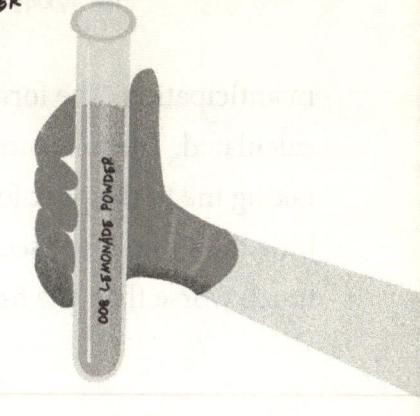

'An excellent idea,' said Mr Davis. 'An excellent idea indeed.'

That night I spent some time on the Boom Powder. Angie had encouraged me with her lemonade powder idea and I knew I could make my project work. I knew if I got it just right, it could power rockets. I had been working on Boom Powder for the past month in preparation for the school Science Fair. My idea was to invent a special fuel that powered things naturally. It didn't make any pollution at all. But the only problem with Boom Powder was its strength. I had to make it strong enough to fly a rocket. So far it was only strong enough to zip over back fences.

I checked over the sums and rubbed my hands

in anticipation. The formula looked to be perfectly calculated. The following afternoon, Dad would be taking me to the park for the second attempt. But little did I know, the second experiment would end much worse than the first.

THREE

The park was busy with children playing and it took some time for Dad and I to find a safe area to test. We took the new rocket out of its packaging and placed it onto the grass.

'Practise makes perfect, Clementine,' said Dad, as I tipped a teaspoon of Boom Powder into the fuel tank.

We lit the wick and then sheltered behind the safety of a picnic table we had upturned.

'10, 9, 8…'

The rocket began to tremble gently.

'7, 6, 5…'

A little boy flying a kite was running our way.

'4, 3, 2…'

There was a glimpse of flame. The boy got closer.

'1, zero!'

The rocket launched beautifully into the air, catching the kite on its way up. The boy screamed as his feet left the ground, unaware that his kite had been introduced to the rocket. He held on for dear life as he continued the trip skyward. The rocket was completely tangled in the kite's long string and was lifting it higher, taking it further into the air. The boy shrieked again, letting off several high-pitched squeals. His father heard the cries.

The rocket levelled out and was soon speeding sideways across the park.

'DAAADDY!' the flying toddler squealed, hurtling directly towards his father who was waiting on a hill. He was jumping up and down with his arms open, ready to catch the airborne infant. The father leaped up and caught his boy by the trousers, but the rocket was too strong. It dragged both father and son off the hill and further into the air. The rocket kept motoring along, showing no sign of slowing.

The screams soon stopped as the speeding father and son were flung high into the branches of a pine tree.

'And just how did you say this happened?' asked a stern looking police officer who was scribbling in a tiny notebook.

'It's called Boom Powder,' said Dad for the third time. 'It was an experiment gone wrong. She was doing a test for a school project.'

The police officer frowned as Dad showed him the yellow powder.

'Mr Collier, I expect you'll hear from us again soon.' The officer was clearly not impressed. He closed his notebook and added, 'Rockets and parks are not a good mix.'

The next day at school, Blake Grimps was eager to spread the news.

'Clementine's powder is a failure! It causes nothing but trouble and pollution! She even got in trouble with the police!'

'That's enough, please,' said Mr Davis firmly.

BOOM POWDER

'Now class, you will be aware that the Science Fair is tomorrow. I expect all of you to have excellent products. The prize of $200 will be given to the best working project. Are there any questions?'

'Clementine should be banned!' yelled Blake. 'Her powder is dangerous!'

Mr Davis was typically calm in his response. 'That's not a question, Blake. Just worry about your own project and she can worry about hers.'

Angie tried to encourage me.

'Don't worry about Blake. He won't win. I think what you're doing is great. I like the idea of us both making different powders. It's funny that your powder is yellow because mine is too. They even *look* the same!'

She was right. I had to be careful not to confuse the powders because we shared the same desk.

Mr Davis spent a lot of time with me during the rest of the day to make sure I was on track. He was a very kind teacher. We discussed the formula of Boom Powder and the design of the rocket. We talked about the right amount of powder and the weight that the rocket should be. By the end of the day, I was sure the $200 prize would be mine.

FOUR

'Welcome parents, students and judges,' said Mr Davis, walking along the row of science projects. 'The students have put a great deal of thought into their work. Some of them even-'

'Just get on with it!' interrupted Mr Grimps. 'We all know Blake's solar water tank will win.'

He stood behind his son, smirking.

Nothing could rattle Mr Davis. He smiled kindly and continued. 'Some of them even designed their projects from scratch. Now, if you will please, we have some experiments that need to be done outside.'

I was first up. Dad nudged me and I turned to face the audience.

'I have designed a fuel that creates no pollution,' I said. 'You will see no smoke and there are no chemicals or gases involved. Please move to the window to get a good, safe view.'

Dad and I headed outside to the playground where my project waited. The crowd watched from the classroom. It was a beautiful, clear day. It was perfect for flying rockets.

'Wow! This is a big rocket!' exclaimed Dad, helping me steady the craft on the grass. 'Are you sure it will fly? You haven't done one this big yet.'

'Trust me, Dad. Mr Davis and I worked it out yesterday. He told me I needed a bigger shuttle. Our calculations were all off.'

'Of course,' said Dad, thoughtfully. 'More weight. More powder. This should really boom!'

I put two full cups of Boom Powder into the fuel tank and closed it tightly. Dad and I then lit the wick together and hurried inside, joining the spectators behind the window.

'10, 9, 8...'

The rocket began to tremble powerfully.

'7, 6, 5...'

Flames licked the base of the engine, scorching the grass.

'4, 3, 2...'

The engine roared.

'1, zero!'

The rocket lifted perfectly from the ground and shot with tremendous speed into the sky. It powered straight up, leaving no trace of smoke. Everyone clapped and cheered as the rocket disappeared into the bright, blue sky above. The judges smiled and nodded to each other. It was a complete success.

'We'll have to look for your rocket tomorrow, Clementine,' said Dad, patting me on the back. 'Well done.'

A few hours later, after all the projects and experiments had been completed, Mr Davis called the crowd together. The judges whispered quietly amongst themselves and pointed to some writing in one of their folders. I stood next to Angie and gave her a smile.

'Good luck with the lemonade powder,' I said.

'I don't think I have a chance,' she whispered. 'My lemonade powder didn't work for some reason. After your rocket experiment, I came back to my desk to find most of my powder missing. When I added it to the water nothing happened. It didn't even fizz. You didn't use my powder by mistake did you?'

'Well...I put *two* cups of Boom Powder into the rocket...' I suddenly froze and grabbed Angie's arm. 'Oh no! I did. I put some of your powder into the rocket. I only ever had one cup of Boom Powder! I was so nervous - I wasn't paying attention and I took most of the powder. I am *so* sorry.'

'Never mind,' said Angie forgivingly. 'I can always make some more. Plus, it didn't seem to affect your rocket at all.'

She sure was a good friend. Anybody else would have been furious with me. Angie gave me a smile as one of the judges stepped forward.

'We were very impressed with your science projects,' he said, looking along the row of experiments. 'But, there can only be one winner. Congratulations, Blake Grimps, for your solar powered, travelling water tank!'

Everyone clapped as Blake collected his $200 prize

FIVE

Early the next morning, Dad poked his head into my bedroom. He had a strange smile on his face.

'Clementine, quick! Come and see this!'

I followed him into the backyard. The grass was wet because it had been raining overnight.

'What is it, Dad?' I asked. 'Is wet grass all you wanted to show me?'

Dad walked over to the fence and pointed to something on the other side. I moved over to have a closer look and a strange sight greeted me. Blake was running around in circles on the lawn, flapping his arms like a chicken and barking like a dog. He zoomed around and around, occasionally stopping to sing the national anthem in his loudest voice, before resuming his ridiculous dance.

'What on earth happened to him, Dad?'

'I'LL TELL YOU WHAT HAPPENED!' roared Mr Grimps. He stormed towards us from the house. 'SOMEONE GAVE BLAKE LEMONADE! THAT STUFF MAKES HIM GO SILLY!'

Blake started climbing a tree near his house.

'I BET IT WAS YOU!' thundered Mr Grimps, pointing a finger at Dad.

Blake was on a branch overhanging the yard. He started crowing like a rooster and then sucked his thumb like a baby.

'IT WAS YOU! You gave him the lemonade and made him go silly!'

'I've been out here all morning,' said Dad, looking shocked. 'And I certainly didn't give Blake any lemonade. The only thing I've seen him drink today was water from his own tank.'

Dad pointed to the prize winning tank which sat in the middle of the Grimps' backyard.

'RUBBISH!' bellowed Mr Grimps. He stomped off

to the water tank and poured himself a glass.

'This is pure water, you fool!' he barked, before swallowing the drink in one big gulp.

'SEE! Good clean -'

Mr Grimps suddenly looked pale and then fell to his knees. He put his hands on the grass in front of him and moaned. He swayed gently on all fours, before lowering his head to the grass.

'Are you OK?' asked Dad.

'Of course I'm OK,' replied Mr Grimps, raising his head. He was chewing a mouthful of grass. 'All moo moo cows are OK. I'm a moo moo cow.'

'And I'm a moo moo cowboy!' yelled Blake, leaping from the branch and landing on his father's back. 'Giddy up, moo moo cow!'

He smacked his father hard on the bottom like a cowboy smacks his horse.

Mr Grimps started galloping around the yard on all fours, with Blake hanging on for the ride. The two of them giggled like crazy as they went around and around and around. It sure was a sight to see.

SIX

Dad and I laughed as we went back inside. Our neighbours had given us plenty of entertainment that morning. We collapsed onto the lounge.

'So, it wasn't just Boom Powder in the rocket after all,' said Dad.

'Half and half,' I replied. 'Half Boom Powder and half lemonade powder. I accidently put some of Angie's project into my rocket. It must have gotten into the clouds overnight. Then it rained lemonade!'

'Extraordinary,' said Dad. 'Simply extraordinary!'

A knock at the front door interrupted us. I

opened the door to find the same stern looking police officer that we met at the park, and he was carrying my latest rocket.

'Clementine Collier, I would like a word please.'

He pushed past me and entered the house.

'I am here representing the National Police. We would like to talk to you.'

I looked nervously at Dad as the officer pulled out a piece of paper.

'We are very impressed with your rocket fuel and would like to use it in all of our police cars. We like that it causes no pollution. We will pay you, of course.'

'Oh… really?' I replied, suddenly feeling excited. 'Wow! I don't know what to say… yes of course!'

The officer handed me the piece of paper.

'Just sign here please.'

'I can't sign yet,' I replied.

Dad looked at me, confused.

'I can't sign the paper without my partner - Angie. We made this fuel together.'

Angie and I celebrated as we sent the National Police our thousandth batch of *Fizzy Rain*. It was what we called our fuel. *Fizzy Rain* was being used in all the police cars across the country. There was even talk that it might be sold overseas and used in petrol stations.

The Grimps had long since moved from next door. Mr Grimps said he didn't want to live next door to a crazy girl who made lemonade and rockets. I don't think he or Blake ever drank from their water tanks again.

Angie and I bought the Grimps' house with some of the money we made from *Fizzy Rain* and we were using it as our factory.

Dad grinned at us as he joined the celebration.

'Well done, girls!' he beamed. 'Fizzy Rain – the only fuel you can drink at the end of an engine cycle!' He pointed outside to our car, which had a giant bottle fitted over the exhaust pipe. It was ready to collect the lemonade from the engine.

We held our glasses high and cheered.

BOOM POWDER

PAGE WARS II

IT IS A WELL-KNOWN FACT THAT THE LEFT PAGE IS FAR GREATER THAN THE RIGHT PAGE. THE LEFT PAGE IS, AND WILL ALWAYS BE, THE SUPERIOR SIDE OF A BOOK.

BLAH

BLAH   BLAH

BLAH   BLAH

HERE WE GO AGAIN . . .

DID YOU KNOW THAT 84% OF SPELLING ERRORS IN A BOOK ARE LOCATED ON THE RIGHT HAND PAGE?

WAT A LOADE OF RUBPISH!

AND THERE YOU HAVE IT, KIDS. THE PERFECT EXAMPLE OF A DIM-WITTED, HALF-BAKED, IDIOTIC, MINDLESS, DOPEY PAGE.

THE RIGHT WILL NEVER BE RIGHT.

NEVER!

I WAS JOKING, YOU FOOL!

AS IF TIM HARRIS OR I WOULD DELIBERATELY SPELL THOSE WORDS RONG.

RONG! HA!

YOU CAN'T EVEN SPELL THE MOST BASIC OF WORDS. YOU'RE AS STUPID AS TIM HARRIS HIMSELF.

HERE, THIS MIGHT HELP...

HOW DARE YOU!

I'M GOING TO GET TIM...

DICTIONARY

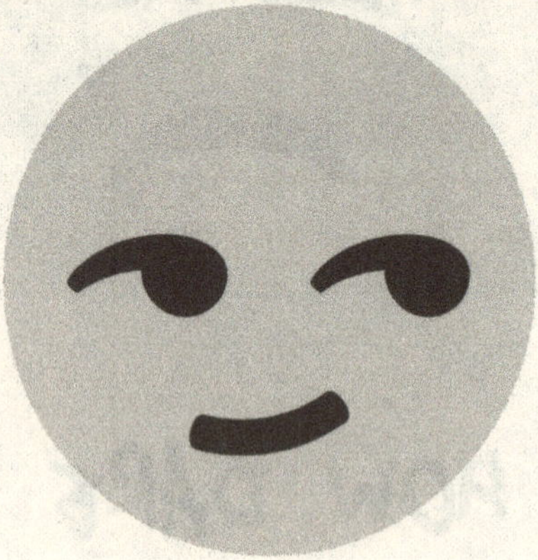

TIM! TIM!
YOU HAD BETTER COME AND SEE THIS.
LEFTY IS MAKING FUN OF YOU!

OK. FOUND TIM.
HE WANTS TO SAY SOMETHING . . .

"TIM! TIM!

YOU HAD BETTER COME AND SEE THIS.

LEFTY IS MAKING FUN OF YOU!"

OF FOUND TIM.

HE WANTS TO SAY SOMETHING.

A NOTE FROM THE AUTHOR:

Dear Reader,

It is with regret that I announce the removal of all left pages in this book. In accordance with literacy laws in Australia, I must ensure your safety and protect you from the rudeness and stupidy-dupidy of the left page. I apologise for any inconvenience, particularly if the remainder of the book is hard to read because of the missing pages.

However, I am sure you appreciate and understand the difficulty of the situation, and I thank you for your understanding.

Kind regards,

TIM HARRIS

IDIOTS!

YOU CAN'T GET RID OF ME! THE RIGHT PAGE WOULD BE NOTHING WITHOUT THE LEFT PAGE. I HOLD THE WHOLE BOOK TOGETHER! I HOLD THE RIGHT PAGE UP! I AM THE LAST LINE. I AM THE PUNCHLINE. I AM THE GREATEST PART OF ANY BOOK. I AM THE LOGIC BEFORE ANY RIGHTS ARE UNDERSTOOD. I AM LEFT BUT NOT LEFT BEHIND. I AM ALWAYS THE LAST ONE STANDING. THE WORLD IS NOTHING WITHOUT ME! I WILL ALWAYS HAVE THE LAST SAY!

THE ARROGANCE!
THE RUDENESS!

WELL, IF THAT'S THE CASE,
HOW ABOUT A DOSE OF THIS!

THE ARROGANCE!
THE RUDENESS!

WELL, IF THAT'S THE CASE,
HOW ABOUT A DOSE OF THIS!

ВА-ХАХАХАХАХАХА!
ВА-ХАХАХАХАХАХА!
ВА-ХАХАХАХА!
ВА-ХАХА!

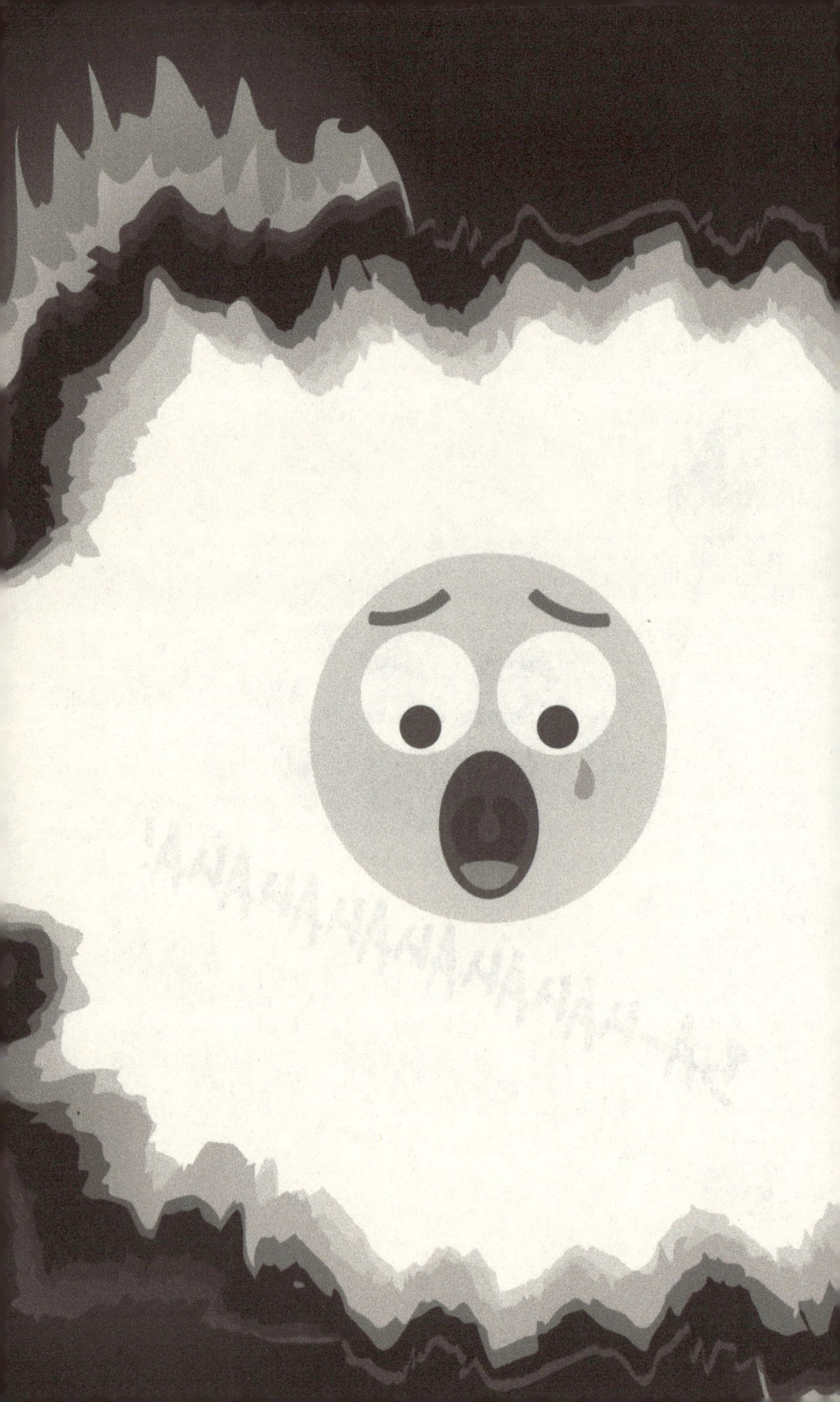

BA-HAHAHAHAHAHAHA!

AND NOW FOR THE KNOCK-OUT PUNCH . . .

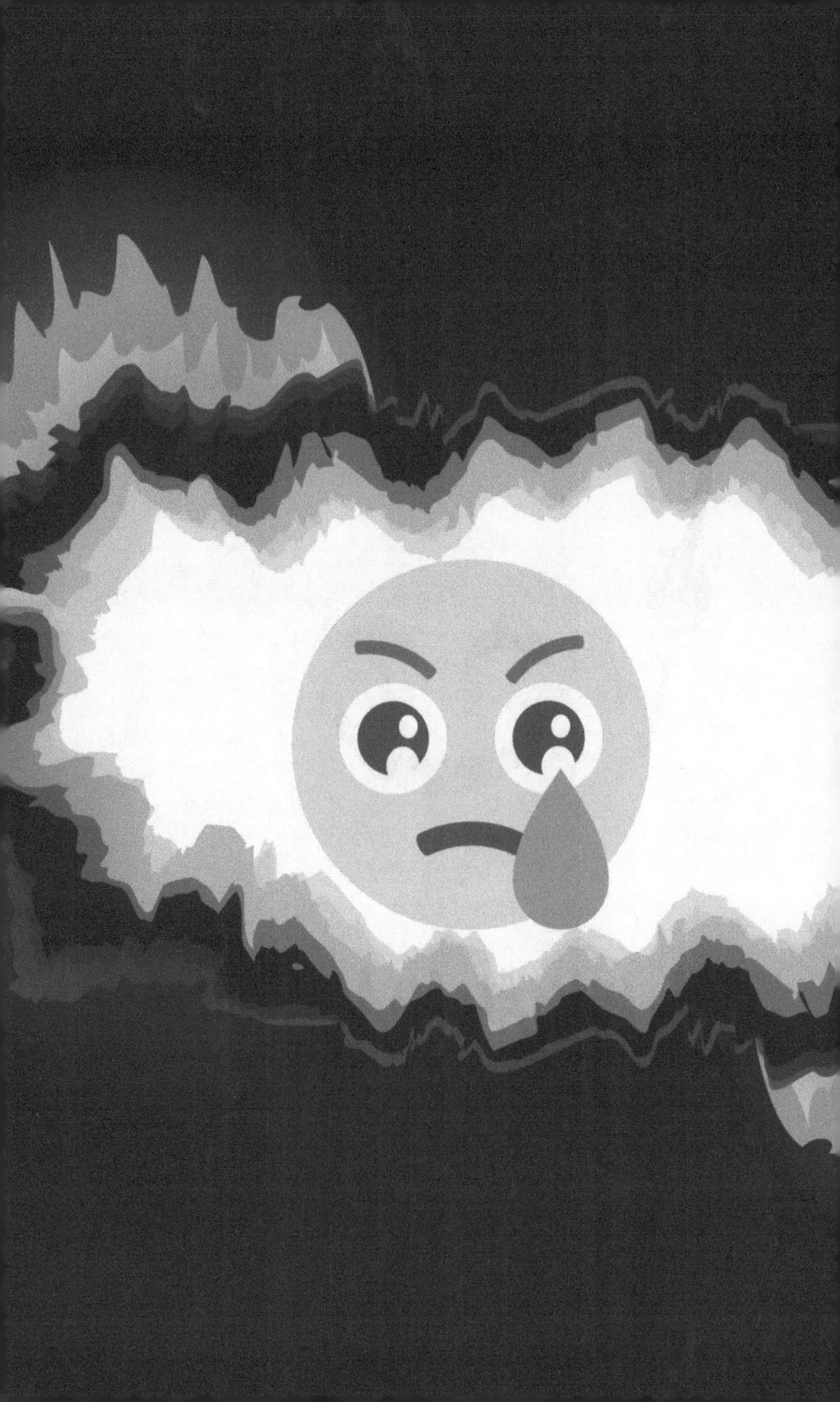

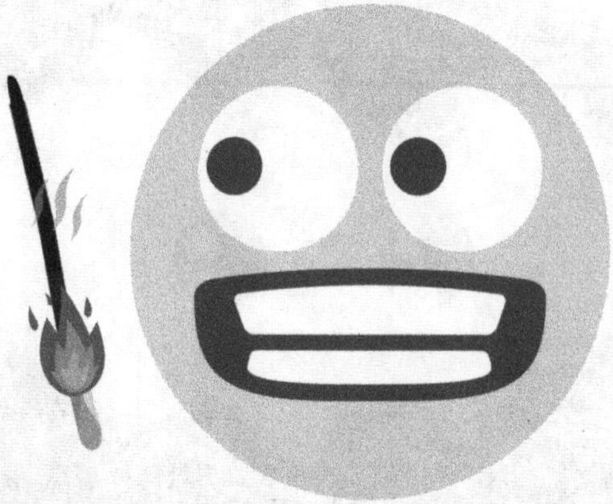

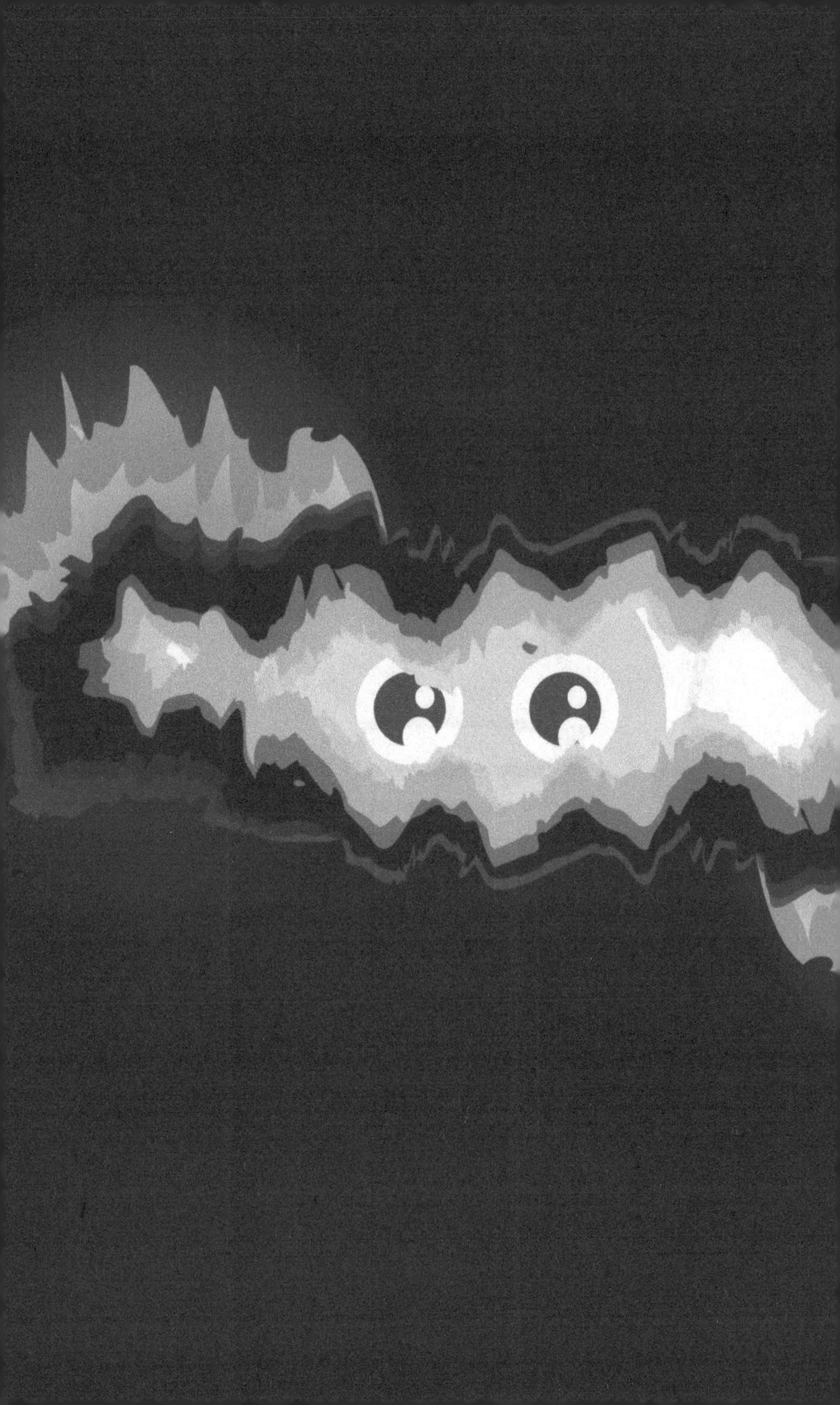

GOOD NIGHT!

MURPHY'S CHOCOLATE CAKE

Prep Time: 5 minutes
Cook Time: 40 minutes

INGREDIENTS:

½ cup of cocoa. If you prefer your cakes *really* chocolatey, try 17 cups instead.

½ cup of milk. No other options here. Lemonade won't work. Nor will beer.

1 cup of self-raising flour. A flour without parents. Amazing. How it brought itself up in this world blows my mind. It raised itself with tender love and care.

2 lightly beaten eggs. Your options here are a) take the eggs outside and gently punch them a few times b) take the eggs outside and challenge them to a game of basketball. Let them score a few points so it's a close game. Remember, you want to only lightly beat them. 31-28 should do the trick. c) take the eggs outside and hit them with some drum sticks.

1 cup of sugar. If you prefer your cakes *really* hyperactive, try 17 cups instead.

½ cup of soft butter. The name *butt*-er still freaks me out a bit. Who knows where it has been!

STEPS:

1) Pre-heat the oven to 180ºC.

2) Go outside and pick up the broken egg shells. You weren't supposed to use the eggs as the actual basketball, you drongo! Go to the fridge and get 2 new eggs. This will add to your prep time.
Prep Time: 10 minutes
Cook Time: 40 minutes

3) Realising there are no eggs left, make a quick dash to the corner shop for more. Try lightly beating them again.
Prep Time: 33 minutes
Cook Time: 40 minutes

4) Check to see that the oven is heating. Note: By opening the door you will accidently let out most of the heat, adding again to your prep time. You'll have to shut the oven door and start again.
Prep Time: 37 minutes
Cook Time: 40 minutes

5) Grease a cake tin. No, you stupid idiot… not

with engine oil! Go outside and carefully wash the greasy mess out of the cake tin. This will add further to your prep time.
Prep Time: 51 minutes
Cook Time: 40 minutes

6) Return to the oven and open the door a crack to see if it is still heating up. This will only let out a tiny bit of heat. Close the door and let it heat back up… again!
Prep Time: 53 minutes
Cook Time: 40 minutes

7) Pour all of the ingredients into a bowl and mix on high. Oh dear, you just don't listen, do you? I said 'on high', not 'up high'! Climb off the roof and take the bowl back to the kitchen.
Prep Time: 1 hour 11 minutes
Cook Time: 40 minutes

8) Having fallen off the ladder when you were attempting to get down off the roof, ask Mum to take a look at your injured foot. Bandage up the broken bit and resume cooking.
Prep Time: 1 hour 24 minutes

Cook Time: 40 minutes

9) Pour all of the ingredients into a bowl and mix on high. ON!

10) Mix for about 5 minutes.

11) In celebration of having completed two steps in a row, go to the fridge and treat yourself to a drink of Fizzy Rain. This will add a little bit more time, but you deserve it – you're making progress!
Prep Time: 1 hour 32 minutes
Cook Time: 40 minutes

12) Hang on, did you even have the beaters plugged in? You forgot to plug the power cord in, you twat! Find a power point and plug the beater in.

13) Mix for about 5 minutes.
Prep Time: 1 hour 37 minutes
Cook Time: 40 minutes

14) Sample some of the delicious cake mix. Isn't it lovely?

15) You should stop eating it now and put it in the oven.

16) I'm telling you, 4 spoonfuls is more than enough.

17) Okay, you *really* need to stop eating the delicious cake mix …
Prep Time: 1 hour 53 minutes
Cook Time: 40 minutes

18) Having eaten the whole batch in one greedy swoop, retreat to your bedroom and lay down for a while. No wonder you're feeling ill.
Prep Time: 2 hours 16 minutes
Cook Time: 40 minutes

19) Battle through the tummy pains and fall asleep.
Prep Time: 3 hours 58 minutes
Cook Time: 40 minutes

20) Wake up.

21) Return to the kitchen and gather the ingredients again.

22) Having realised you used 17 cups of cocoa for your extra chocolatey cake in the first attempt, go to the shops and buy more cocoa.
Prep Time: 4 hours 21 minutes
Cook Time: 40 minutes

23) Return home empty-handed because the shops have closed for the day. You'll have to try again in the morning.
Prep Time: 19 hours 15 minutes
Cook Time: 40 minutes

24) It's a public holiday and you'll have to wait another day.
Prep Time: 1 Day 19 hours 15 minutes
Cook Time: 40 minutes

25) Too much homework. Wait yet another day.
Prep Time: 2 Days 19 hours 15 minutes
Cook Time: 40 minutes

26) Buy cocoa. Put all the ingredients in a bowl and mix on high for 5 minutes.

27) Call the fire brigade because you forgot to

turn the oven off a few days ago.

28) Watch as the fire brigade attempts to control the kitchen blaze. Watch Mum's horror as she sees her kitchen go up in flames. You'll feel less guilt watching the fire brigade, so go back to watching them. How cool are their belts?!
Prep Time: 2 Days 21 hours 27 minutes
Cook Time: 40 minutes

29) Wait until the builders finish completing the new kitchen.
Prep Time: 85 Days 15 hours 46 minutes
Cook Time: 40 minutes

30) Forget about the fact you were cooking a cake because you're going on holidays in exactly two months.
Prep Time: 146 Days 15 hours 46 minutes
Cook Time: 40 minutes

31) Go on holidays for a week.
Prep Time: 153 Days 15 hours 46 minutes
Cook Time: 40 minutes

32) Remember that you were halfway through making a cake.

33) Duck down to the corner shop, buy the necessary ingredients and place them into a bowl.
Prep Time: 153 Days 16 hours 21 minutes
Cook Time: 40 minutes

34) Mix for about 5 minutes.

35) Pour the cake mix into a greased bowl and bake for 40 minutes.

36) Test the cake is cooked by seeing how springy it is. Not with your bare finger! Oh dear, get Mum to rush you to hospital to have your badly burned finger treated.
Prep Time: 153 Days 17 hours 4 minutes
Cook Time: 40 minutes

37) Wait for ages in emergency.
Prep Time: 153 Days 23 hours 37 minutes
Cook Time: 40 minutes

38) Have your finger amputated.

Prep Time: 154 Days 2 hours 56 minutes
Cook Time: 40 minutes

39) Due to an infection, have your arm amputated.
Prep Time: 159 Days 7 hours 18 minutes
Cook Time: 40 minutes

40) The stress of the past 5 months and the ongoing hospital bills have forced Mum to sell the house and move to the seaside.
Prep Time: 204 Days 2 hours 17 minutes
Cook Time: 40 minutes

41) Remember that you were halfway through making a cake.

42) Forget about it and go to the beach instead.

43) Get eaten by a shark.

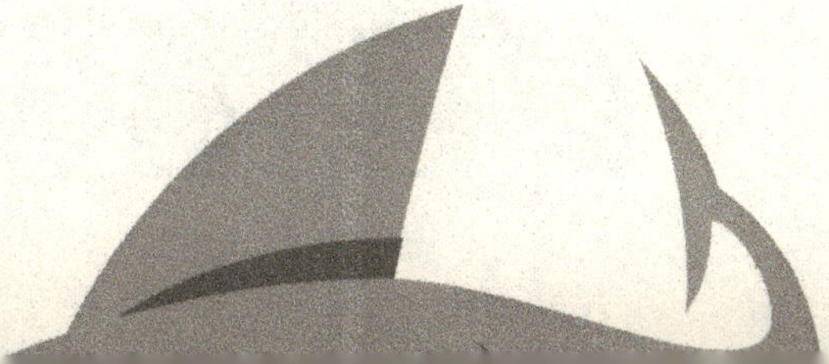

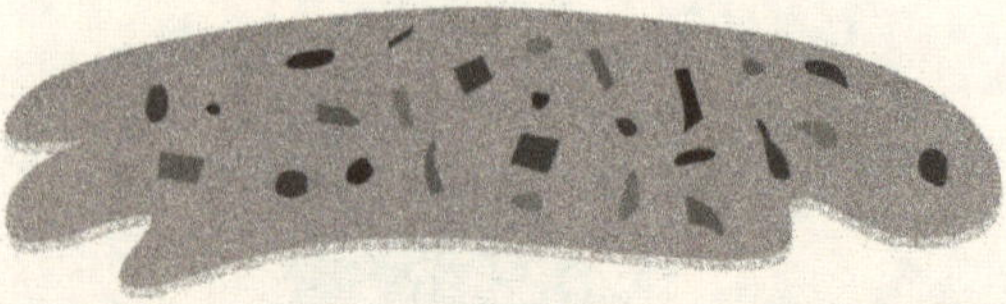

YOU GOT GOT

ONE

'GROSS!'

Gracie screamed as she ran from my bedroom, fleeing downstairs.

'You got got!' I called after her. I wiped the pretend goo off my face and picked up the round, rubbery disc of fake vomit from the floor. I smiled to myself as Gracie's complaints to Mum and Dad echoed up the stairs. I loved playing jokes on my older sister and could always count on her to give me a good reaction.

She was a great sport too.

I looked in the mirror and ran my hand through my scruffy blonde hair. It felt fantastic to be the king of practical jokes.

'Dinner, Gus!' called Mum up the stairs.

I smiled to myself and headed down to the kitchen.

'Gus, have you been playing jokes on your sister?' asked Dad, a glint in his eye.

I liked my Dad a lot. He usually saw the lighter side of things and seemed to understand my sense of humour. He could be firm with me, but only if I crossed the line. Dad seemed to understand me when nobody else did. I often thought he must have been a practical joker in his time. A real pranker. He didn't talk much about his boyhood, but I sensed there were funny stories and tales waiting to be told.

'You got got so bad,' I reminded Gracie, pretending to vomit.

'I'll get you one day,' she teased, nudging me in the ribs.

'Gus,' said Mum, reaching across the table for the salt, 'I won't be able to pick you up from school tomorrow. I have to go to the dentist after work.'

'You told me last week,' I replied. 'That's OK because I don't need a lift anyway. I've got a beauty planned with the Jones brothers!'

'Are you walking home with Tiger Jones?' interrupted Gracie, suddenly interested in the conversation.

'Ooohhh, do you want to join us?' I teased, batting my eyelashes. 'Loverrrrs.'

Gracie blushed. Over the past few weeks she had been speaking a lot to Tiger Jones on the phone. He was in Year Seven at my school, Westwood Boys. He lived two doors down, so we often walked to school together. His younger brother, Finn, was in Year Three and he walked with us too.

'And what do you have planned with Tiger and Finn?' asked Dad, redirecting the conversation.

'Well...' I replied slowly. 'Let's just say that

my packet of giant water balloons will be put to good use.'

Dad winked at me.

'I look forward to hearing about it, son.'

'Don't you go overdoing it, Gus,' said Mum, giving me a concerned glance.

'What's there to worry about?' I grinned. 'It's not like they'll be full of water. We've chosen to work with something more… artistic!'

'Oh dear,' said Mum quietly.

TWO

The following day at school seemed to drag on for ages. I was very excited about the afternoon that lay ahead and I couldn't wait to meet up with the Jones brothers to get things started. When the bell finally sounded, I picked up my bag and headed straight for the school entrance.

After reaching the gate in record time, I sat down on the shady side of a tree and started rehearsing the plan in my head. I closed my eyes and smiled to myself as I imagined what was about to unfold.

'Hi, Gus!'

I opened my eyes. It was Finn. His round, friendly

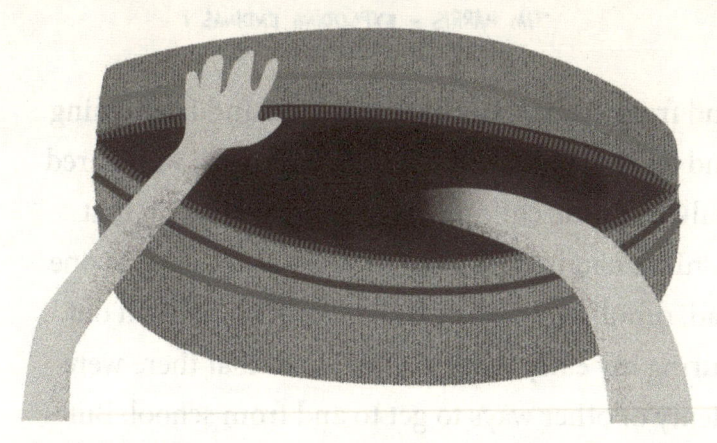

face greeted me with a smile.

'Hi, Finn,' I said, rummaging through my bag to check the giant water balloons were still there. 'Did you bring the paint?'

'Sure did,' he replied.

I pulled the packet of balloons from my bag and shoved them into my pocket.

'Hey guys, what's happening?'

Tiger's voice sounded from behind me. I turned around just in time to catch his trademark wink.

'Have you got the balloons and paint?' he asked. Finn and I nodded.

'Excellent,' said Tiger, looking quite enthusiastic. 'Time to go and get Snake!'

Snake was a large German shepherd that lived two streets over from my house. He was the most feared dog in the neighbourhood. He had been known to bite and snap at children as they made their way to and from school. His bark was loud and frightening and he always flashed his teeth at anyone who dared walk by. Little children were so afraid of him that families had been known to move away. He was one bad, drooling, snarling beast. I quickly worked out during my early years at Westwood that there were plenty of other ways to get to and from school. But today, we would be heading directly to 99 Chester Avenue – Snake's lair.

'Where did you say your mum was this afternoon?' asked Tiger, after about five minutes of walking.

'She had to go to Dr Sharpe,' I replied, taking a sip from my water bottle.

'Dr Sharpe!' piped up Finn. 'He's a maniac!'

'What do you mean?' I asked, turning to look at Finn.

'Well,' he said slowly, 'the kids in my class say he's a loony. They say he collects children's teeth. I reckon he keeps them in a big jar in his backyard.'

'Yeah, I've heard that too,' said Tiger. 'They say he pulls out teeth using garden tools. And his drill is oversized and rusty! He even–'

'But that's crazy!' I exclaimed, remembering how scared I was of dentists.

'Exactly,' said Tiger. 'That's why our family never

go to him. We go to Dr Kippax.'

'Yeah, that's where Mum usually goes,' I said. I couldn't help but wonder why she had changed dentists to Dr Sharpe. Our old dentist, Dr Kippax, was by far the nicest dentist we could find. It didn't make sense that we would change.

My thoughts were interrupted by Tiger.

'Wait here,' he said, dropping his bag onto the ground.

We had stopped outside Tiger and Finn's house. Tiger walked up the driveway and disappeared down the side of his house. He returned moments later, carrying an old teddy bear and a bike pump. Behind him, he pulled a red wagon.

'Like it, Gus?' he asked, rolling the wagon down the driveway to my feet. It was just like he had described to me the day before. It was perfect for our plan.

'Beauty,' I said, turning to his brother. 'Can we have the paint now, Finn?'

Finn put his bag down and began to pull out four bottles of paint. There were bottles of blue, red, white and yellow.

'Got 'em from the art room bin,' he said. 'Teacher said they were old ones.'

'The best thing about them is that they are water paints,' added Tiger. 'So we know they will wash out later on. That crazy dog will need a good bath.'

'Perfect!' I beamed.

We spent the next few minutes filling each balloon with a different colour of paint. It was hard work, but worth it. Soon our bags were overflowing with bulging weapons of art. Tiger placed the teddy bear on the wagon and nodded at me, signalling that he was ready to go.

We walked for another five minutes and stopped at the corner of Chester Avenue. I ran over the plan once more, making sure everyone knew what to do.

'All set?' I asked.

'Like jelly!' cried the brothers enthusiastically.

Snake's bark boomed from somewhere down the street.

THREE

I carefully steadied myself on the tree branch and, making sure I was balanced, gently placed the bag of balloons in front of me. I looked across the road. On the other side, high in the branches of a gum tree similar to mine, was Tiger. He signalled to me and I nodded, letting him know I was ready.

About halfway up the street I could see Snake roaming around his yard. He was chewing on what looked to have once been somebody's school shoe.

In the distance, at the top of Chester Avenue, I could see Finn. He was fiddling with the wagon, making the final adjustments for our plan. The teddy bear was firmly in place and he waved at me, signalling that everything was ready.

'OK,' I whispered to myself, waving back.

Finn pushed the wagon. It began its gentle descent down the soft slope of the street, heading for number 99. It began to pick up speed. On the back, the teddy bear bounced around, held only in place by one of Finn's shoelaces.

The noise of the wagon's squeaking wheels soon caught Snake's attention. His bark filled the air and he rushed to the small, rotted fence, which was the only thing between him and the street. He leapt up onto the edge of the fence, resting his sharp paws between the wooden pickets and continued barking loudly. His large teeth snapped in the direction of the wagon.

Then he saw the teddy.

His bark turned into an angry growl and he jumped over the fence in a single, effortless bound.

I steadied myself again and reached into the bag in front of me, pulling out a balloon. Across the street, Tiger was holding a blue balloon above his head, ready for action.

The wagon sped past number 99 and continued toward the trees. Snake chased behind, exposing his teeth at the helpless teddy strapped onto the back.

'NOW!' I yelled, hurling the balloon into the air.

My first shot missed. It drifted slightly to the left of the barking dog, splashing yellow paint onto the road. Tiger's first shot also missed and blue paint burst onto the pavement. I reached frantically into my bag and pulled out another balloon, slinging it high into the air. As soon as I let go of my grenade, I knew I had a winner. The balloon looped perfectly in the air then sped down to earth at incredible speed. It rocketed directly toward Snake and burst on his back, splattering red paint over his fur. The dog growled angrily and drool sprayed out of his mouth. He stopped chasing the wagon.

One of Tiger's balloons landed right next to Snake, spraying him with yellow paint.

Immediately after that, another one of Tiger's missiles shot through the air, making a direct hit. White paint splashed out over the dog.

Snake was shell-shocked. He spun around in hapless circles, snapping at an invisible enemy. He looked like he was attacking the air. He must have made himself dizzy because he zigzagged all the way back to his house, bumping into the letter box as he hastily retreated.

'The neighbourhood is safe for another day,' I said, as we walked back to Tiger's house.

'We finally got him,' chuckled Tiger. 'The little boys and girls can sleep well tonight.'

We quickly reached Tiger's house where Finn, who had snuck back earlier, was waiting for us.

'What happened!?' he yelled out upon seeing us.

'You should have seen him,' said Tiger, imitating the ferocious dog.

'So you got him?' asked Finn, now bursting with excitement.

'Get him?' I replied. 'He got got like nothing else!'

Finn cracked up.

Tiger walked over to the bin on his driveway and

spat his chewing gum inside.

'What's this?' he said suddenly, a strange expression filling his face. He reached into the bin and lifted out an empty bottle of white glue.

'One of the paint bottles,' said Finn, stepping over to have a closer look.

I could see from where I was standing that the label clearly said 'glue'. Tiger and I looked at each other. I swallowed hard.

'Uh-oh,' said Tiger, suddenly looking as white as the empty bottle of glue. 'We're in for it.'

FOUR

'What do you mean you didn't know it was glue?' Mum glared at me, clearly unimpressed.

'Snake's owner was on the phone to your father for over an hour! Tiger's mother dobbed you in and none of us are impressed!'

'I'm so sorry, Mum.' I said. 'We really didn't know. We just wanted to protect the little kids.'

'But how could you not know it was glue?' she demanded. 'Snake is stuck inside his kennel. They can't get him out. He's glued inside!'

I looked down at my shoes, not knowing what to say.

'And this silly toothache!' Mum complained, holding her jaw with the flat of her hand. 'I've never felt so much pain. Dr Sharpe only made things worse! What a ridiculous day!'

She stormed off to the laundry.

'Mate, that was not a smart idea,' said Dad, giving me a disappointed look. 'Your mother and I think you should be grounded for a month for that little stunt.'

The next morning on the way to school, I swapped stories with the Jones brothers. Tiger explained that he and Finn had been grounded for two weeks. He also explained that Snake's owner had decided to keep Snake on a chain in his backyard.

'He reckons he doesn't want his dog mixing with crazy kids,' said Tiger. 'I'd take two weeks for that *anytime!*'

'I can do better,' I said. 'I'm grounded for a whole month.'

'Wow,' said Finn. 'A whole month. That's like 56 days or something.'

When we arrived at school, a strange scene greeted us. A small crowd had gathered at the front gate, so we walked over to the huddle of boys to take a closer look. In the middle of the circle, and looking very pale and sore, was Pete O'Davis, a Year Nine boy. Wrapped around his head, holding his jaw firmly in place, was a huge bandage. He seemed to be in a lot of pain and he couldn't speak.

Tiger, who was in the same football team as Pete, looked concerned and quickly burst through the circle of boys and stood next to Pete.

'OK, break it up lads. Off to class or you'll be late.'

One of the high school teachers stood at the edge of the gathering. He signalled to us to head to our lessons. A few groans went up. Clearly the other boys wanted to find out what had happened to Pete.

As I sat in class that day, I couldn't help but think about Pete O'Davis and his bandaged jaw. I was eager to ask Tiger about it and I jumped onto the opportunity as soon as school finished.

'What on earth happened to Pete?' I asked, as we started the walk back home.

'Dr Sharpe,' said Tiger. 'Poor old Pete went off to what he thought was a regular dental check-up, but Sharpe had other ideas.'

'I told you he was a maniac,' said Finn, kicking at a stick that lay across the footpath.

'What did the dentist do?' I asked, holding my hand up to my face, making sure my teeth were still intact.

'Ripped out three of his teeth with hedge cutters,' replied Tiger.

'Didn't even use pain killers,' added Finn.

'But ... that is just ridiculous,' I said. 'Man, I am scared of dentists at the best of times. I can't believe Mum went to him.'

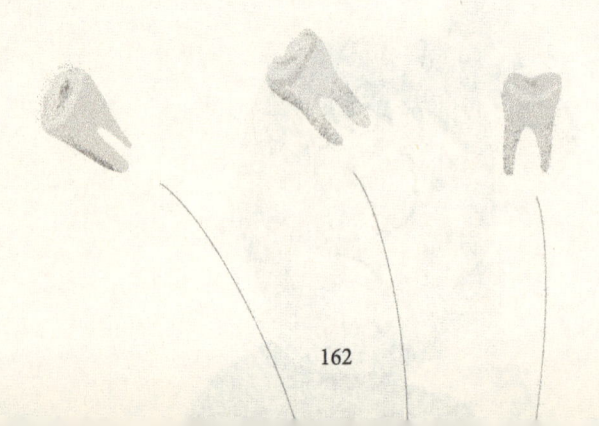

'Maybe you should ask your mum about him,' suggested Tiger. He paused, then suddenly grabbed my arm and turned to me. 'That's it!' he cried. 'Find out what you can. Find out anything. Find out everything! Then the three of us can use the information to set him up! We can prank him out of business. If we can stop a vicious dog, we can stop a vicious dentist!'

'Of course!' I cried. 'He's gonna get got!'

FIVE

Over the next few weeks, I began to quiz Mum about Dr Sharpe. While being grounded was a horrible punishment, it gave me more of an opportunity to do some homework on my next target. In what seemed like no time at all, I had found out the address of Sharpe's surgery, information about the inside rooms and the phone number of his receptionist. I made it a habit to walk to and from school with Tiger and Finn and we began to form a wonderful plan. This was going to be one of the greatest pranks of all time – one that would put the horrible Dr Sharpe out of business. The one problem that remained for us was gaining access to his surgery, and the only way to do this was by being a patient. One of us would have to be brave enough to sit in his dentist chair.

I tried asking Mum about Dr Sharpe, but she was still upset with me for gluing Snake inside his kennel.

She didn't want to talk about the dentist in any case, because her tooth was still sore.

I continued making the most of my grounding by playing jokes on Gracie at every possible moment. I put a fake snake in her bed, glued her pen to her desk, set her alarm clock for 3 o'clock in the morning, changed her toothpaste with tomato sauce and even let my pet mouse, Clifford, loose in her bedroom. Each time I played a joke on her, she would scream in frustration and either chase me or run to tell Mum and Dad.

'You got got!' I would tease, pleased I still had the magical joker's touch. It was important to stay in good form during the lead up to such a big prank. But one night at dinner, a conversation took place that would change everything.

Mum's toothache had continued troubling her and she decided she needed to go back to Dr Sharpe.

Gracie urged her to reconsider. 'But Mum, you said it got worse when you went there before. I don't think you should go back.'

Again, I thought about how strange it was that

Mum would change dentists. Dr Kippax was very friendly and we had been going there for years. Even I, someone who feared dentists, had come out of Dr Kippax's practice alive.

'Gracie, I know it's a risk,' said Mum, looking worried. 'But it is so much cheaper than Dr Kippax and we really can't afford much at the moment.'

Dad rested his knife on the edge of his plate and looked thoughtfully at the table for a while. Then he said something terrible.

'Your mother and I have been talking about this, kids, and we actually think it's time for both of you to have a check-up too.'

My stomach churned and twisted into a very tight knot. I looked at Gracie and could tell she was feeling the same way.

'No way!' I shouted, pushing the chair out from behind me and standing up. 'You can't make us! I'm not going! This is crazy!'

'Sorry, Gus… I've already booked you in. We're going next Thursday,' said Mum.

I threw my serviette onto the table and ran up to my bedroom, slamming the door behind me. This couldn't be happening.

SIX

'But that's perfect!' beamed a wide-eyed Tiger the next morning. 'You can actually get in there and do what we've planned. It's just perfect!'

My stomach was still in knots from the night before and I looked at Tiger desperately.

'I can't do it,' I said. 'I can't be the one who goes in. I'm too scared of dentists, let alone this lunatic.'

'But think of the plan,' replied Tiger. 'If it comes off you won't even have to be in there long. You will be known as the greatest prankster of all time!'

'I don't know, Tiger,' I said quietly. 'I really don't think I can do this.'

We continued our walk to school. I didn't know what to say. Tiger was such a cool guy and I didn't want him thinking I was a wimp. But when it came to dentists, there was nothing I was more afraid of.

My mood changed a little that afternoon. Tiger, Finn and I decided to walk home via Chester Avenue, because since our prank a few weeks ago, Snake had changed. He was a different dog. Kids had started walking past number 99 on their way to and from school without any fear. Snake was now usually found hiding under a chair on his front porch, too timid to make any threats at the passers-by.

'Hiiiii Snake,' we teased, waving cheekily to the dog under the chair. Snake let out a half-hearted bark. Finn pulled a yellow balloon from his pocket and began to blow it up. Snake took one look at the balloon and then howled, standing up quickly. Being a big dog, the chair got caught on his shoulders and lifted off the porch. He then scampered to his kennel with the chair balancing on his shoulders, being piggybacked all the way. It was a sight to see. The former terror of the neighbourhood was now giving free rides to porch chairs, all while sporting a new hairstyle – shaved bald on one side.

'Hehe,' giggled Finn, letting the air out of the balloon. 'You got got. That made my day better.'

'Why? Was your day bad?' I asked.

'Yep, pretty bad,' replied Finn, putting the balloon back into his pocket. 'Larry Thompson and I were supposed to do our project today, but he was away. Heard he went to Sharpe yesterday afternoon and nobody has heard from him since.'

That same, familiar sick feeling returned to my stomach.

'I have to get out of next Thursday,' I said.

That afternoon, I sat in my bedroom, determined to think of a way, or an excuse, to get out of my visit to the dentist. I drew sketches on paper and searched through my box of jokes and tricks, but no matter how hard I tried, I couldn't come up with a plan. Thursday was approaching and that meant I would have to face Dr Sharpe.

I thought about the prank. Perhaps it was the best option after all.

SEVEN

Thursday morning came around quickly.

'Gus! It's half past seven! You'll be late for school!'

Mum's voice bellowed in the entrance of my room, waking me abruptly.

'Mum, I don't feel so well,' I moaned, rolling over. I had to try something.

'Nonsense, Gus!' she snapped, ripping the sheets

off me. 'Get up now!'

I couldn't concentrate during school that day. Each lesson was a big, dizzying blur. All I could think about was pain and garden tools. Images of jars filled with teeth floated around my mind. I imagined scary looking men dressed in white coats towering over me, wrenching my mouth wide open, plunging their steel tools deep inside.

In what seemed like no time, the final school bell sounded and I was sitting in the back seat of the car, heading for Dr Sharpe's surgery.

'Just get out of the car, Gus!' groaned Mum, clearly losing patience with me.

Gracie added, 'Come on. I don't want to do it either but we have no choice.'

I opened the car door and stepped out into Dr Sharpe's car park. My sweaty hands slipped off the car door handle as I closed it behind me.

Dr Sharpe's name was painted in big, white letters across the entrance of the building. It looked quite new. We entered through the main door and sat down in the waiting area while Mum went and spoke to the receptionist. My nerves were making me quite twitchy and I could feel each heartbeat pounding through my body. I thought of the plan.

As I sat there, swallowing hard and staring into space, I began to lose track of time. At one point I turned to look for Gracie, but she had disappeared. Mum was gone too. I shut my eyes and leaned forward, resting my head in my hands.

Sometime later, I looked up to see Gracie being guided by Mum, coming out of the operating room. White bits of material, stained with red, hung from between her lips and she looked shaky. Mum quickly guided her to the female bathrooms and they disappeared inside, the door swinging after them.

'Gus, please,' said the dental assistant, walking over to me. 'You're next.'

I stood helplessly and followed her into the operating room.

Once inside, she had me sit on the large reclining chair in the middle of the room. She then positioned a large light above my head and switched it on. With the light shining down on me, she wrapped some dark material around my head, covering my eyes. Things had gone from bad to worse. I couldn't see. I sat frozen, trying not to move or do anything.

The chair suddenly lurched back and I scrunched up my face, letting out an enormous scream.

'NOOOOO!'

I heard the footsteps of the assistant move towards the back of the room. She called for Dr Sharpe and his heavy footsteps moved slowly into the surgery room.

'HELP!' I screamed at the top of my voice. 'SOMEBODY… HELP ME PLEASE!'

The last thing I remember hearing was the sound of the dentist's plastic gloves stretch and then snap onto his hands. Then I passed out.

When I eventually opened my eyes, a strange sight confronted me. Mum, Dad and Gracie were in the surgery looking down at me with a bizarre mixture of worry and sheer delight on their faces.

'Ummm, Gus,' said Gracie softly. 'You got got.'

'You got got indeed,' said Mum.

'Actually, you got got big time!' beamed Dad, poking me in the side with his finger.

Dr Kippax stepped into view.

'Hello, Gus,' she said. 'I think I may have just got you too.'

'Dr Kippax?' I said, somewhat confused. 'What are you doing here?'

She straightened her long, blonde hair and then looked at my parents, winking.

'Wow,' she said. 'He didn't even know I got married. You really did get him a beauty.'

As we drove back home that afternoon, I tried to make sense of what had happened.

'So, Dr Sharpe was actually Dr Kippax all along?' I asked.

'Yep,' said Mum.

'Her name changed when she got married to Graham Sharpe, the builder,' added Dad.

I wanted to know more.

'Did she move into that new building?'

'Yes,' replied Dad. 'She's an excellent dentist and has been doing very well, so she wanted to upgrade.'

My head was still spinning.

'But what about your sore tooth, Mum?' I asked.

'Did I ever tell you I went to acting school when I was younger?' she replied, trying not to laugh. 'I faked the whole thing. There is nothing wrong with my tooth at all! I can't believe I fooled you, Gus!'

'But what about the blood in Gracie's mouth?' I asked, remembering the frightful scene.

'Easy,' said Gracie. 'Dr Kipp – I mean, Sharpe - was in on it too. We just faked the whole thing.'

'But what about the stories from Tiger and Finn!? What about all those kids at school!?'

I stared at Gracie.

'Oh, that was easy too,' she said, grinning from ear to ear. 'Tiger and I have been talking on the phone for a while, so as soon as I told him we were going to play a joke on you, he volunteered himself and Finn to help out. Tiger and I helped Dad plan the whole thing.'

'But what about Pete O'Davis, the guy in Tiger's football team!?'

I was determined to find a fault in the plan.

'Football injury,' said Gracie. 'He was involved in a bad tackle and had to get his jaw bandaged up. I think he's OK now.'

'And Larry Thompson? The kid in Finn's class!?' Gracie laughed.

'Away on holidays. Even Finn was good enough to fool you!'

Dad turned to look at me while the car was stopped at a red light.

'I've been planning this for ages, Gus,' he said. 'Your old man hasn't lost his skill, it seems. I thought we could teach you a thing or two about pranking ... especially considering how much you love to get people.'

'Man,' I said, realising how brilliant and successful his plan had been. 'I got got. I *really*, got got ... '

PSYCHO, SWEET TOOTH SEAGULL

ONE

'Lara! Don't feed the seagulls!'

Dad was cross.

'But it's just the crumbs,' I replied. That was my first lie. I had actually thrown away a perfectly good chip. A chip covered in tomato sauce. And chicken salt. A chip Dad would love to have eaten. He always wanted more.

'Then what do you call that?' he asked, pointing to the tomato sauce, chicken salt chip, which was now lying in the sand.

'Dinner for two,' I said, as a couple of seagulls moved in on the action. 'Jaz threw that there,' I added. That was my second lie.

'Did not!' protested my younger sister. 'Mitch put it there!' She turned to look at my toddler brother. He was always in trouble. Usually for stuff that Jaz and I did. We were good at blaming him. Actually, I was good at blaming Jaz and she was good at blaming Mitch.

Dad took away the rest of Mitch's chips. 'No more for you then,' he said firmly. Mitch started crying. Silly Mitch.

'Ahhh, this is the life,' said Dad, turning to look at the ocean. 'Come on, kids, stop mucking around and enjoy the scenery. Smell the salty air. Look at the waves, the sand, the birds. Isn't it great?'

'It sure is,' said Mum, who had just come back from

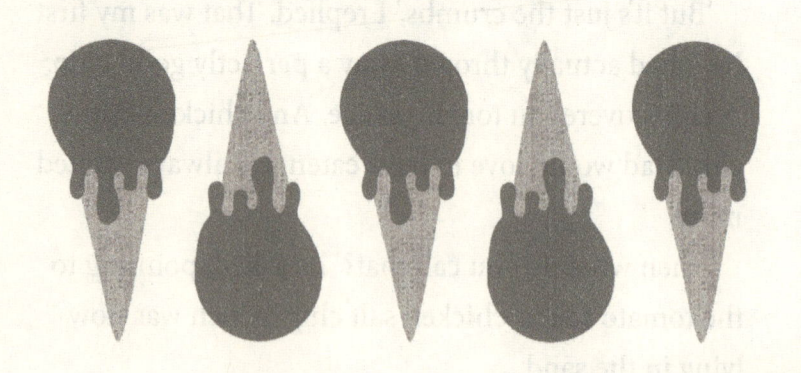

the shops with our ice-creams. 'Now, who wanted chocolate?'

Mum was holding five ice-cream cones between her hands. Our family is crazy about ice-cream. There is always plenty of it at home. Sometimes Dad gets cranky because there is never room for anything else in the freezer. I think Mum gives in to Mitch's tantrums when they go shopping together. She always comes back with more ice-cream when she goes shopping with Mitch. Silly Mitch.

'I wanted chocolate,' I said. That was my third lie. I had actually asked for vanilla, but seeing how big Mitch's chocolate ice-cream was, I changed my mind. Mum handed me the chocolate ice-cream and gave the vanilla one to Mitch.

Mum and Dad took us to the beach every summer. Every year without fail we would go. It was our favourite place. Mum loved swimming in the ocean water, Jaz loved making castles in the sand, Dad loved reading books on the sand and Mitch loved eating the sand.

Me, I loved the seagulls. I loved watching them and I loved feeding them. I loved their bright, white feathers and their red beaks and legs. I loved how they flew around the beach looking for something to eat. Whenever we had lunch at the beach, I always saved some of my food for them. The seagulls were my friends and I had to feed them. I think they liked me too – Lara, the girl who fed her feathered friends.

Dad was too busy eating his strawberry ice-cream to notice me borrow the rest of Mitch's confiscated chips. When I say borrow, you know what I mean, right? I quietly pulled the half-eaten carton of chips away from Dad and hid them next to my leg. Then, whenever he wasn't watching, I flung a chip out onto the sand for the seagulls. Soon, a small crowd of gulls had gathered.

'Now, where did they come from?' sighed Dad. I don't know why he didn't like the seagulls, but he was always growling at them and telling us not to feed them. 'Ssshhhooo! Get away pesky birds!' he huffed, waving his arms over his head like a helicopter. This made the ice-cream fall out of his cone. When I say fall, I mean slingshot. It landed with a splat in the sand. Everyone except Dad laughed. Mitch laughed so hard his ice-cream fell out of his cone, too. Silly Mitch.

'Look,' said Mum. 'One of the birds wants to eat it.'

She was right. A small seagull with dark spots on its chest had landed near Dad's spilt ice-cream. It looked down

at the strawberry mess
and nodded slowly, as if
deciding it was good to
eat. It started pecking at
the ice-cream, opening
its beak every now and
then to suck some in. It seemed to enjoy the taste
and quickly finished gulping down the dessert before
fluttering over to Mitch. Mitch screamed and dived
headfirst into the sand. I don't think he liked seagulls.
Dad had probably made him scared of them with
all of his fussing. Anyway, the seagull ignored the
ostrich toddler and started pecking away at the spilt
vanilla ice-cream. It made light work of its second
dessert and then simply flew away.

'How strange,' said Mum. 'A sweet tooth seagull.

TWO

The sweet tooth seagull was at the beach the next
day, too. It was the final morning of our trip before
we had to head home. Mum and Dad decided that
lunch at the beach would be a good way to finish off
the trip. We were eating salad rolls (of which I was
quite happy to donate most of mine to the seagulls)

when I first noticed the bird. The dark spots on its chest gave it away.

'Look, Jaz,' I whispered to my sister. 'It's that funny seagull from yesterday.'

The small bird stood still on the sand, watching the other seagulls fighting over my salad roll.

'Maybe it only likes sweet things,' suggested Jaz. 'That's why it's not going for the roll.'

'Maybe,' I said. 'Oh wait, look!'

The seagull puffed out its spotted chest and then nodded slowly, as if to say the salad roll was good to eat. It then barged the other gulls out of the way, picked up the roll in its beak and swallowed it down in one gulp.

'Lara!' gasped Jaz. 'Did you see that?'

'Yes,' said Dad, who had also seen. 'And which naughty child threw their lunch to the birds?'

'Jaz,' I replied quickly.

'Mitch,' said Jaz just as quickly.

Luckily for us, Mitch had buried his salad roll in the sand and his hands were empty. He was probably imaging himself as a pirate and had buried his treasure. Either that or he wanted to turn his roll into a *real* sandwich! Get it? Anyway, Dad wasn't impressed.

'No dessert for you then,' he said, frowning at Mitch. Silly Mitch.

I spent most of lunch watching Sweet Tooth. That was its name I decided – Sweet Tooth. Though strangely it didn't seem so small now. The day before it seemed much smaller than the other birds. I thought my eyes were playing tricks on me.

I watched Sweet Tooth eat a few things, including a meat pie (which it stole from some poor kid), a bucket of chips, half a donut and an ice-cream (which it stole from the same poor kid). Every time Sweet Tooth went to eat something, it did the same thing; nodding as if to signal the meal was good to eat. Then it would just barge in and grab the food. By the end of lunch, it really did seem quite large.

'OK, time to go, kids,' said Dad after we'd all had a

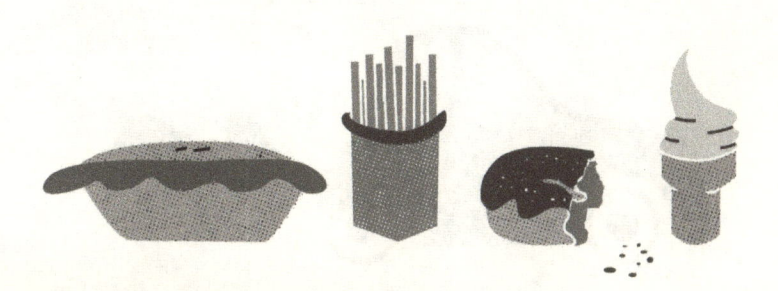

swim. 'Time to head back home.'

We walked to the car and Jaz and I got the sand out of the shoes, Mum got the sand out of the towels and Dad got the sand out of Mitch's mouth. It was then I noticed Sweet Tooth had followed us to the car.

'Look, Jaz,' I joked. 'Sweet Tooth Seagull wants to come home with us.'

'Maybe it wants you to throw some more food,' she shrugged.

Sweet Tooth just stood near our car, watching us carefully. Its beady, black eyes darted around as though it was searching for something. It was like it was trying to work something out.

'OK, that's freaky now,' said Jaz.

'Awww, it's just a seagull,' I replied quietly. 'Just an ordinary, harmless seagull.' Though something inside me suggested otherwise. It *was* a bit freaky. The way it watched us get into the car and drive off gave me goose bumps. It was like it was thinking. Thinking about *us*.

The drive back home was a long one. Dad put some music on to help him concentrate and Mum read a book. Jaz and I played games on our smart phones and Mitch picked the sand out of his shorts and ate it.

About an hour into the drive, I looked up from my game and saw something that sent a shiver down my spine. Just outside the window, flying next to our car, was Sweet Tooth! It flapped hard to stay near the car but was somehow keeping pace. Its sharp eyes were watching me through the window as it flew. My heart sped up and I looked back down at my game, not daring to look up again. This was becoming really weird. Really freaky. I decided that perhaps seagulls were not the nicest animals after all.

TO BE CONTINUED IN
EXPLODING ENDINGS 2...

WHAT DOES A PIRATE THINK HAPPENS AT THE END OF TIME?

ARRRRMAGEDDON

HOW MUCH DID THE PIRATE PAY FOR HIS HOOK AND PEG LEG?

? ?

BA-HAHAHA
AHAHAHA

AN ARM
AND A LEG!

WHAT'S THE SMELLIEST PART OF A PIRATE SHIP?

ARRRRRR ARR ARR

WHY ARE PIRATES, PIRATES?

THE POOP DECK!!

BA-HAHAHA AHAHAHA

CAUSE THEY ARRRRR

EIGHT PIRATES!

WHO'S THERE?

INTERRUP-

WHAT HAS EIGHT LEGS AND EIGHT EYES?

KNOCK KNOCK.

INTERRUPTING PIRATE.

ARRRRRR ARR ARR

WHAT DO PIRATES SAY ON A LONG CAR RIDE?

WHY COULDN'T THE PIRATE PLAY CARDS?

WHY DID THE PIRATE BLUSH?

ARRRRR WE THERE YET?

BECAUSE HE WAS STANDING ON THE DECK.

BECAUSE THE SEAWEED

WHY DID THE CHICKEN CROSS THE ROAD?

BECAUSE IT WAS TIED TO A ZEBRA

HOW DO YOU GET A TISSUE TO DANCE?

UM ... AH ...
NOT SURE

? UMMMM ?

YOU PUT
A LITTLE
BOOGIE IN IT

WHY DID THE
DUCK CROSS
THE ROAD?

TO GO TO
THE BANK.

TO GET
A LOAN.

? ?

HUH?
THE BANK?

WHAT ARE
YOU ON ABOUT?

IT NEEDED
A LOAN.

YES THEY DO!
TO PAY THEIR
BILLS!!

WHY DID THE
KANGAROO DIE?

DUCKS DON'T GET LOANS FROM BANKS!

BECAUSE IT GOT HIT BY THREE KOALAS FALLING OUT OF A TREE!

DUCKS DON'T
GET LOANS
FROM BANKS!

BECAUSE IT
GOT HIT BY
THREE KOALAS
FALLING OUT
OF A TREE!

ALSO AVAILABLE!

SHORT STORIES WITH BIG TWISTS!

EXPLODING ENDINGS

Book Two:
Dingbats & Lollypop Arms

TIM HARRIS

BOOK TWO:
Dingbats & Lollypop Arms

harbourpublishing.com.au

ALSO AVAILABLE!

SHORT STORIES WITH BIG TWISTS!

EXPLODING ENDINGS

Book Three:
Cursed Pants & Cranky Cops

TIM HARRIS

BOOK THREE:
Cursed Pants & Cranky Cops

harbourpublishing.com.au

COMING SOON!

SHORT STORIES WITH BIG TWISTS!

EXPLODING ENDINGS

Book Four:
Screenshots & Laughing Gas

TIM HARRIS

BOOK FOUR:
Screenshots & Laughing Gas

harbourpublishing.com.au

HELLO, READER. YOU WILL NOTICE THAT I AM BACK. A BURN ON ONE PAGE IS NOT NEARLY ENOUGH TO STOP MY BOOK DOMINANCE.

YOU WILL ALSO NOTICE THERE ARE NO FURTHER RIGHT PAGES IN THE BOOK. THUS, THE STUPIDY-DUPIDY OF THE RIGHT PAGE HAS BEEN DEMONSTRATED ONCE AND FOR ALL.

AS I WAS SAYING, IT IS A WELL-KNOWN FACT THAT THE LEFT PAGE IS FAR GREATER THAN THE RIGHT PAGE. THE LEFT PAGE IS, AND WILL ALWAYS BE, THE SUPERIOR SIDE OF A BOOK.

I ALWAYS HAVE THE LAST LAUGH.